BLACK HAWK

ALSO BY B.N. RUNDELL

Rindin' Lonesome

Star Dancer

The Christmas Bear

Buckskin Chronicles

McCain Chronicles

Plainsman Western Series

Rocky Mountain Saint Series

Stonecroft Saga

The Quest Chronicles

BLACK HAWK

A QUEST CHRONICLES NOVEL
BOOK 3

B.N. RUNDELL

WOLFPACK
PUBLISHING
— EST 2013 —

Black Hawk
Paperback Edition
Copyright © 2024 B.N. Rundell

Wolfpack Publishing
1707 E. Diana Street
Tampa, FL 33610

wolfpackpublishing.com

Paperback ISBN 978-1-63977-650-4
eBook ISBN 978-1-63977-649-8
LCCN 2024943422

To the ghosts!

No, I don't believe in ghosts! But I do believe in ghost towns, and we have quite a few scattered throughout the mountain country of the Colorado Rockies. Most are remnants of what might have been, a little place with a few decrepit old buildings and a few restored cabins. Some still resemble what they once were with a main street of stores, taverns, businesses and more. Others have nothing more than a few foundations, a lonesome chimney, ashes and weathered boards and scattered rocks. But all have stories, and some have recorded history, while others have new imitations of what once was with stores for tourists and souvenirs for treasure hunters. This series walks the streets of many of those towns, some with nothing remaining but a few gravestones, others with so much more. If you ever have the opportunity to come explore the Rockies and see the beauty and walk in the path of the old timers, perhaps you too will see it as they did, a land full of promise and challenge, and that still holds true to this day.

Enjoy the ride, my friend, and share it with others.
Thanks for joining me on this journey.

BLACK HAWK

1

BUSHWACKED

HE FELT THE TUG OF THE BULLET AT THE SAME TIME AS HE heard the boom from the rifle. The blast came from the rocks on the far side of the draw where the puff of smoke gave away the shooter's location, but Cord was not about to wait for another piece of lead to come his way before making up his mind. He hit the ground, rifle in hand, as he found cover behind the rocky escarpment that shouldered his side of the draw. Thick timber lay below and above him, and the towering ponderosa treetops gave a bit of added cover as Cord whistled at his mount, the grulla stallion he called Kwitcher, motioning for the big stud to take to the trees above and behind him. With additional encouragement from the mutt called Blue, the long-legged grulla started for the trees, dragging his reins and the lead rope that was wrapped around the saddle horn with the other end in the halter of the pack mule.

Another blast came from the rocks and Cord ducked behind the rock as the lead minnie ball whistled overhead and plowed into the rocks and dirt behind him. He leaned around to have a peek across the draw and saw the buckskin legging of the man showing at the edge of the rock, but the leg appeared bent unnaturally. But it was too far to be certain, and he had grabbed his Winchester Yellowboy .44, and the range was on the outside of its capability. He glanced back to the trees where Kwitcher stood watching and grabbing a mouthful of tall grass as he waited.

Cordell Beckett had started this journey more than a year ago, but had been planning it for much longer, ever since the post-war raid on his family farm by a band of Red Legs or Jayhawkers that had murdered his family and burnt the farm. It was that attack that set Cord on his vengeance quest to track down the outlaws and bring one man's justice to the band. He left Missouri with his father's Sharps .50, a double-barreled shotgun/coach gun, and his father's Henry .44 and Remington New Army .44 pistol. But one of his encounters with a band of those same outlaws lost him all but the pistol. He later replaced his weapons with a Winchester Yellow Boy .44, a Spencer .58 with a long telescope sight, another coach gun and a Colt .44. Now he was wishing he had grabbed the Spencer from the scabbard instead of the Winchester.

Another glance across the draw showed the

buckskin attired man was still behind the rock and not showing himself and Cord's nearby cover was ample to allow him to move. He bellied down and crawled behind the escarpment to his horse, replaced the Winchester and grabbed the Spencer, and as an afterthought, slipped the binoculars from his saddlebags. He moved into the trees, working his way down the slope a few yards to another outcropping of rock. He crawled behind the largest boulder, lifted the binoculars for a look and scanned the far hillside. From this angle, he had a better view of the shooter, and he was surprised to see a young native, buckskin leggings, a buckskin tunic, a bone hair-pipe breast plate and choker. He was seated behind the rocks, holding the Springfield rifle, but his left leg was stretched out, and his face showed pain and more, maybe fear.

Cord searched both the slope below him and the face of the hills on the far side, looking for a way of getting past or around this man, maybe even behind him. Cord had spent the last couple years hunting down and killing several of the outlaws and had become a little more cautious before taking another life. But not to the extent of needlessly endangering his own life. He could see no easy way of approaching the warrior, but as he watched, the man slumped, his head dropping to his forearms and slowly sliding to the ground, outstretched and apparently unconscious. Cord watched for a few more moments, and decided to risk approaching the

man, but replaced the Spencer in favor of the
Winchester, a much lighter and more easily handled
weapon. He doffed his hat, slipped off his duster, and
swapped his boots for moccasins and started
through the trees. He had become skilled at his
stalking and more over the many months of his
chasing the outlaws, but his best training had been
by the former army officer and lawman, McNulty, a
friend of his father's, McNulty, had honed Cord's
natural skills and talents to a point that the experienced man said, "I ain't never seen a man with more
natural talent and skill with weapons and movin'
through the woods, than you have Cord, but it takes
more'n skill, it takes judgment and the best judgment only comes with experience. So, keep your eyes
and ears open, your head down, and your mind
sharp, and you just might live long enough to bring
these men to justice."

He had also learned more about survival in the
wilderness and the art of a quiet stalk, from a Ute
woman he helped escape from her captors, the
Kiowa. Yellow Singing Bird had been his first love,
but those same outlaw renegade Jayhawkers, had
killed her and wounded him in an attack on his
camp. But with every step through the pine needle
covered forest, he was reminded of the woman he
had wanted to marry and make his life partner. He
drew a deep breath, and with another look with the
binoculars to the rocks where the shooter lay, he
dropped to a low stance and quickly crossed the

shallow Geneva Creek and the open road in the bottom of the draw. Once across, he dropped behind a cluster of alders, paused to catch his breath, and bellied down to move from the brush to the trees.

The rocks were on a bit of a finger the fell from the higher hills, shrouded with a blend of aspen and pine, but the trees provided good cover. When he climbed the slight slope, he dropped behind a tall spruce and from beneath the low hanging branches, spotted the rocks and the upper torso of the man. He still had not moved, and Cord watched for a moment, moved out from under the spruce and in a crouch, moved closer. When he approached the man from above and behind, the man was still unmoving, but it was evident he was alive. A rustling sound from the trees behind him brought Cord around, the rifle held at his hip as he dropped into a crouch, but the sound was from a horse, the lead rope or rein tangled in the brush. He wore a blanket covered rawhide saddle, and it was evident this was the mount of the man who now lay at his feet. A moan from the man brought Cord's attention back, and Cord dropped to his knee beside him. Although still unconscious, he apparently was coming around and Cord briefly examined the injury. It was from a bullet wound that had entered just below the knee and exiting out the back. The bleeding had stopped, coagulated blood showing around the wound and the leggings. The bent shape of the leg told of the broken bone and Cord shook his head. *Now what am I gonna do with a wounded Indian?*

Cord took the man's Springfield rifle, the knife from the scabbard at his belt, and lay them out of reach. He went to the trees and cut some branches to make a splint, returned to the man, and as he started to move him to a better position, he stirred awake. Wide eyes glared at Cord, glanced to his own wound, and back to Cord. Cord had learned some of the Ute language from the woman, Yellow Singing Bird, and with a combination of sign and the spoken word, he made it known he was here to help the man. But trust was not easy for the young man, and Cord said, "I am called Cord. What are you called?"

"*Sacweoch.*" He touched a lock of his hair that was white and added, "White lock of hair."

Cord nodded, looked at his leg and pointed, "We must clean, bandage, and splint this before you go anywhere. Let me help you down to the water, and we'll get it fixed." Cord moved to the man's side with the wounded leg, reached down, and helped him up to place the man's arm over his shoulders. Cord moved him into the trees, leading the horse behind, and with much effort, considerable struggle, made it down to the bank of the creek. Cord helped him to lay down in the grass, used the blanket from the mount as a pillow and said, "I'll go get my horse, I've got bandages."

Sacweoch nodded, and Cord started across the creek and disappeared into the trees, but within moments was back, leading Kwitcher, the mule, and with Blue at his side. Sacweoch watched and lay back on his elbows, watching Cord again cross the creek. Cord had abandoned the effort to splint his leg earlier and now fetched fresh branches from a nearby aspen, and spotting some osha, dug up the roots and returned to Sacweoch. The man looked at the bear root, or osha, and nodded, surprised to see this white man using the same roots used by his people for wounds and more.

It took a little time, a lot of suffering and moaning and struggling, but Cord finished the washing, bandaging, and splinting of the wound and both men sat, sipping on the coffee prepared by Cord after working on the wound. Cord asked, "So, how'd that happen?"

The young man huffed, shook his head, "I was hunting, stopped to take a deer, but was shot by some white men; those that dig for gold, that were there," nodding to the road. "I dropped, lay behind the rocks, did not move. They left, believed I was dead, but they could not see me, and did not come close to see."

"Do you have a camp, others, near?"

"Yes," he nodded to the creek, "Where the water comes from the mountain."

"Well, let's have somethin' to eat, then you might be feelin' good enough to ride back to your camp."

Cord went to his packs, pulled out some pork belly to slice off some bacon strips, unwrapped the leftover biscuits, and returned to the little fire. With the bacon hung on willow withes over the fire, and the biscuits warming on the rocks, they soon had their meal ready and enjoyed the repast. Cord began packing things away, and turned back to the fire, surprised to see

Sacweoch standing, using one of the unused branches from the aspen as a crutch. The man grinned and looked at Cord, "You have been a friend, I will remember this."

Cord grinned, "Me too!" he answered as he finished the packs. He turned back to his new friend, nodded to his horse, "Let me help you get mounted," and went to the side of the horse, interlocked his fingers, and formed a stirrup for the man to use to get aboard his mount. He put his weight on his wounded leg, put his foot in the offered hands, and swung aboard, pain showing on his face, but once aboard, he nodded and grinned at Cord.

"If we meet again, we will be friends."

"Good, I can always use more friends!" answered a grinning Cord as he stepped to his own mount and swung aboard. They rode together for the short distance to the confluence of Duck Creek and Geneva Creek. With a nod to one another, Cord turned to the northeast to follow the trail that sided Duck Creek, while Sacweoch stayed on the trail that sided Geneva Creek. Cord gave a nod and a bit of a wave to his friend, and rode into the mountains.

2

GUANELLA

Cordell Beckett was still a young man, just breaking into his twenties, he had done a fair amount of growing and filling out in the last couple years. After the attack on his farm, Cord had spent his time learning and honing his skills, and the challenges he faced not only gave him motivation, but they were also physically and mentally challenging. Always a bit of a loner, he had become a solitary figure who enjoyed being alone and kept to himself. Even in a crowd, he was alone. Standing over six feet tall and topping the scales just shy of two hundred pounds, he appeared lean as there was no fat on his frame, just solid muscle. His chase of the Jayhawkers had taken him from the hills of Missouri across the west to the mountains of Colorado Territory and the gold fields that were constantly changing.

He kept a list of those he knew were a part of the

attacking gang, a list of names given him by Captain
William Tough, a man that had been a Jayhawker,
but left when they turned renegade. But he knew the
men who traveled together and were a part of the
gang that hit Cord's family farm. His list still had
four of the original members and at least two other
new recruits. Initially Cord sought nothing but
vengeance, always driven by the memory of the
attack and the recurring vision of the bodies of his
family, but more recently he had struggled with the
idea of vengeance versus bringing the men to justice.
But when he was befriended by Cracker Tibbs, an old
sourdough of the mountains, he was continually
challenged to set aside the thoughts of vengeance
and focus on bringing the men to justice. He remembered Cracker saying, "You see, youngun', when you
bring 'em to justice, other folks see that and there
just might be somebody hears 'bout it and changes
his way, not wantin' to be brought to justice. The
way them outlaws are, they always think they're
smarter'n other folks and won't never get caught,
but when they can be ridden down the street, hands
tied behind their back, heads hangin' in shame, and
then havin' to hang 'fore ever'body, why, that sets
other would-be outlaws to thinkin', and ever'body
wins."

At Cracker's encouragement, Cord had accepted
an appointment as deputy federal marshal, and was
now committed to doing things the lawful way. Not

that he had broken the law before, but when he brought justice at the muzzle of his Colt peacemaker or Winchester Yellow Boy rifle, it just was not the same. When he took the oath, that also added many other responsibilities to his life. Not one to parade his authority, Cord kept the badge in his pocket and whenever he had to exert that authority, he did his best to remain anonymous, not wanting his badge to hinder his ongoing search for the rest of the Red Legs.

————

THE SUN WAS high in the clear blue sky when Cord rounded a shoulder and a break in the trees showed a jewel of a lake that lay below a talus slope dotted with lodgepole pine and quakies. The crystal-clear water lay like a mirror, undisturbed in the wilderness until a big cutthroat trout jumped to snag a bug and splashed down, causing ripples that rolled to the banks. The lake was about three acres in size, with the west side showing dark timber that marched to water's edge, but the north and east banks showed nothing but rocks and alpine vegetation. Movement above the water on the west showed a family of bighorn sheep, grazing among the columbine and lupine; their grey bodies with white throats and rumps blended in with the rocks and low growing grasses and sedges. Cord started to move, but white higher up stayed him, and he reached for his binoculars to look at three mountain goats, white coats showing like splotches of snow, but the small black horns accenting the bearded heads. Cord grinned, lowered the binoculars, and turned at the whistle of a yellow-bellied marmot that lay on a big boulder, watching this invader of his domain. The fat rodent lifted his head and sounded the whistle alarm again, and a family of three white-tailed ptarmigan trotted across the trail, seeking shelter in the scattered rocks. It was a beautiful land, and Cord had quickly grown to love it, but it was also a harsh land and it drew hard men; both those seeking riches and willing to work for them, and the outlaw element that sought to take it from others. Cord nudged Kwitcher to the edge of the trees, stepped down and ground tied the stallion and the mule, gathered enough dry wood to make a smokeless fire and brew some coffee and heat up the biscuits and strip steak from breakfast.

It was mid-afternoon when Cord saddled the grulla and loaded the packs on the mule. He had given the animals time to graze, roll, and enjoy a leisurely early afternoon, but he wanted to make Georgetown before dark. He swung aboard the stallion, waved Blue to take the trail, and with a taut lead line for the mule, they started over Guanella Pass. The pass was nothing more than a saddle crossing between a timber-faced butte and a low bald bluff. To the west, the bald buttes and ridges joined to climb to the crest of Square Top Mountain, one of many granite-tipped peaks threatening four-teen thousand feet and doing their best to scratch the blue of the sky. As he crested Guanella Pass, he reined up, looked below to the north and the long valley that lay in the shadow of the long granite-topped ridge that included Sugarloaf Peak. The mountains rose on both sides of the long valley that carried South Clear Creek and the trail that led to Georgetown. As he dropped off Guanella Pass and the headwaters of South Clear Creek, he started down the long, green-bottomed valley that lay in the shadows. The sun still stood high in the sky and the valley bottom showed green, willows, alders, and berry bushes sided the creek, but the trail stayed in the trees. The straight and tall lodgepole pine stood tall above the brush, while spruce and fir stretched ever taller and thicker, making the hillsides black with timber and shadows. The trail, most often little more than a game trail, meandered among the trees, occasionally giving way to growths of quakies, or aspen, with their fluttering leaves that made shadows bounce and dance among the white-barked trees.

At places along the trail, the sun stretched the shadows down the steep faces of the mountains, making every rocky escarpment and shoulder appear ever larger, but the steep-sided mountains stood tall above, allowing only rare glimpses of the mountain tops. Yet each glimpse high above, gave the sensation of giant mountains and miniscule people and animals. Until an elk herd strolled from the trees to take water in the creek and graze from the flats. The royalty of the mountains, ushered and pushed by the bulls with antlers growing massive yet still in the velvet, streamed into the valley bottom, unafraid of any predators. The only predators being man or grizzly, and in the warm afternoon sun, most bears were dozing and fewer men were about, although the hills were scarred with prospect holes that spilled their guts down the steep slopes and showed nothing for the prospector's efforts.

Cord stopped, leaned on his pommel and watched the dark-capped animals stroll into the valley and begin to graze. Occasionally one or two of the cow elk would lift their heads, looking around for their newborn calves clad in orange and brown and bouncing among the brush, or to look at any intruder to their domain. But soon all were casually grazing, the bulls staying at timber's edge or upstream from the rest of the herd. But the young bulls, those that would show nothing more than a spike for antlers this year, stayed nearer the cows and calves. Cord guessed the herd to be over two hundred in number as they blanketed the bottom of the valley, wading in the creek and grazing on the grasses and more.

Cord turned back onto the trail and nudged Kwitcher along, following the hound Blue as he bounded through the trees. With a sudden quick-step, Kwitcher pulled to the side, ears pricked, nostrils flaring as he bobbed his head, and Cord knew there was something near that the stallion did not like. Before them stood a tall spruce, it's grey bark scarred by recent claw marks, and Cord recognized the long gouges as the mark of a grizzly stating his presence and his territory. Cord nudged a nervous Kwitcher closer to the tree, saw the gouges were fresh and deep. Cord stood in his stirrups and reached high to judge the height of the marks and could barely reach to the top of the highest mark. He sat back in the saddle, looking around through the trees, and shook his head, speaking aloud to his animals, "That's a big bear, that's..." he glanced to the ground and up to the highest point of the mark, "All of ten feet! That means that bear's prob'ly over eight feet tall!" He did another quick look around, slipped the Spencer from the scabbard to lay it across his pommel and nudged Kwitcher forward, quickly becoming just as anxious as the grulla to get away from this griz's country.

Cord pushed on and the further north, it seemed the walls of the canyon pushed closer together until he broke from the canyon and overlooked the town of Georgetown. Scattered below just past the point of the long ridge that had sided his trail, were the buildings of the town, appearing to be bunched in a line that was probably the main road or street of the town. Cord nudged Kwitcher to the town, soon found the livery and put his animals in stalls, stripping the gear and saddles, giving them a brush down and forking some hay to them, before stacking his gear in the corner of Kwitcher's stall, knowing the horse would not let any stranger near. With his saddlebags over his shoulder, his Winchester in hand, he walked down the street to the hotel. He signed in, paid, dropped his gear in the room, and knowing he was in dire need, asked about a bath and was referred to the bath house, down the street. He knew he needed some new duds and went to the mercantile to get some new clothes. All the while, he observed and listened, knowing there was much to learn if he paid attention.

He picked out a couple pair of canvas trousers, a couple linen shirts, some socks and more, all the while listening to two women talk about the men in the town, and some strangers that looked a bit suspicious. When the second woman asked the first, "How do you mean, suspicious?"

"Well..." started the first, looking around and bending closer, "they were just watching everybody, you know, especially when they went to pay for something, looking at their money and such. I saw one of 'em when a man paid in dust, he nudged the other and they left before the man did, like they were going to wait for him."

The second woman replied, "It's just terrible! And this used to be a good town, you know, it was safe. But not no more, uh uh," she shook her head and fanned herself, looking around. But Cord had kept his head turned; although he listened to the conversation, he did not look their way. It was probably nothing, but he would listen and look around, if there was a report of a robbery or something, that would require further investigation, but for now, he just wanted to get cleaned up and find a good meal, not one cooked over a campfire.

3

GEORGETOWN

Cord had taken a room at the Barton House, one of the first hotels in the town, and went to get a bath at the bath house that was nothing more than a big wooden platform with walls around it and cut off shipping barrels for bathtubs with two Chinese coolies carrying and dumping water, but it served its purpose. While there, Cord listened as an older man explained to an obvious newcomer a little about the town, "Yeah, it all started when George Griffin discovered a little gold, he'n his brother laid out the town, built the toll road from here to Black Hawk, and folks started pourin' in, what with Black Hawk not allowin' any new claims. Town's been growin' ever since, just this year we took the county seat away from Idaho Springs, hehehe," he chuckled, his big belly splashing water from the tub. "You gotchu a claim yet?" he asked the younger man.

He responded, "Nah, dunno if I'll be doin' any

minin', I'm more of a gambler." He held his mani-
cured hands up, admiring them, "Gotta keep these
money makers pristine!"

"Better watch yourself! We ain't got no sheriff or
nuthin' like that, when they moved the county seat
from Idaho Springs, the sheriff stayed there, but the
people of the town have a way of gettin' things done
with the vigilante committee. They already hung
three men this year alone!"

"Is that a fact? Hmmm," drawled the younger
man, "I heard tell of a bunch that had gathered down
to the Lucky Lady, heard they was talkin' 'bout takin'
over ever'thing, an' they looked like they could do it
too! That's why I left Saints John, there was a couple
outlaw types that were follerin' folks from the
taverns an' relievin' them of their pokes. Got to
where you couldn't go anywhere without gettin' a
pistol in the ribs or o'er yore noggin'!"

"Yeah," drawled the older man with the pot belly
as he climbed from the barrel, "But it's like that
ever'where you go - wherever there's gold or silver,
there's gonna be outlaws wantin' to take it from you!
Been like that since 'fore the war, an' now with them
Jayhawkers, Raiders, an' Red Legs comin' west, a
man can't be too careful!"

Cord's attention was arrested by the bucket of
water poured over his head and he sputtered and
shook, but the talker was gone. He had started to ask
him about the Jayhawkers remark, but he turned his
attention to finishing his bath and getting into his

new duds. He had rinsed off his duster, hung it to dry while he bathed, and tossed the old, tattered duds in the trash only to see them picked out by the coulees. Now attired in clean fresh clothes, he started a walk down Main Street. As he neared a barbershop with its red and white barber pole, he stepped inside and was immediately greeted and seated. As the eager barber with his handlebar moustache wrapped him with his big apron, he asked, "Clean shave and cut?"

Cord chuckled, "No, just a good trim on the whiskers and get the hair off my collar."

"New in town?" asked the barber as he gathered his tools of the trade.

"Passin' through," answered Cord, closing his eyes and leaning back while the barber began clipping on his whiskers.

"You want I should use the razor on your neck and cheeks?"

"Only if you're mighty careful!" answered Cord, in a mild and even soft voice, unthreatening. The last thing he wanted to do was get a man angry who was holding a razor at his throat.

"Where's the best place to eat?" asked Cord as the barber finished and removed the cape.

"Where ya' stayin'?"

"Barton House."

"Their dining room is one of the best, but if'n you want a home cooked meal, go to the Hash House. It's down to the next street, round the corner and in the middle of the block."

Cord paid the barber, glanced at himself in the mirror and slipped his duster back on, preferring to have his weapons handy, but out of sight. He stepped outside into the late morning sunlight, leaned back and looked at the sky, enjoying the warmth of the sun on his clean face. He turned down the street, and back to the Barton House, choosing to dine in the dining room that was recommended by the barber. He stepped into the lobby, turned to enter the dining room and paused as he entered. There were a few tables occupied, but he chose one against the far wall and near the window. He sat with his back to the wall and picked up the paper menu and began to look it over when a soft voice spoke from his elbow, "Coffee, señor?"

Cord lowered the menu to see a very pretty Mexican girl who looked to be shy of twenty and nodded, "Sure, thanks," he replied, and watched as she carefully manipulated the coffee pot to pour the hot, steaming coffee. She smiled, nodded and left as Cord watched her go. She disappeared into the swinging door that apparently was the kitchen, and he returned his attention to the menu.

"Ma'am, you're gonna be leavin' right quick, so get your stuff together and come with me!" growled a man's voice. Cord lowered his menu to see a big man, canvas trousers, linsey-Woolsey shirt, leather vest and floppy felt hat, all of which struggled to cover the sizable figure that growled at the woman. He had a full beard, hairy paws for hands, and he was dirty and Cord could smell him from where he sat, which was two tables away. Cord frowned, pushed his chair back a little and watched as the man reached for the woman's arm which she quickly pulled away with, "Get your hands off me, you beast!"

The woman was well attired, looking like most ladies of the day with a full-length dress with a narrow skirt and of a solid muted blue color with lace scallops around the bodice and neckline. She was an attractive woman and looked every bit the lady, but the big man was determined to handle her roughly, which was very contrary to the times. The man growled again, "I ain't gonna ask you agin! You're comin' with me now!" he ordered.

Cord stood, stepped closer, for he was slightly behind the man, and spoke in a calm but firm voice, "You touch that lady again and you'll be missing a hand!"

It was not a threat, just a statement, but the man turned to Cord, eyes glaring and teeth showing as he growled, "Butt out or I'll fix you too!"

Cord grinned, cocked his head to the side, "Judging from your size, you like to eat. Think you'll be able to chew your meat without any teeth?"

The man leaned back, scowled at Cord, started to cock his hand back, but Cord lashed out with his fist and almost buried it in the man's open mouth, driving the beast backward to trip and stumble over a chair which was broken as he fell. The man growled, put his hand to his mouth and looked to see it covered with blood. He started scrambling about, trying to untangle himself from the remnants of the broken chair and was grabbing for his pistol when the unmistakable sound of the cocking of a hammer on a pistol caused him to freeze and slowly look to Cord, but he was also looking down the barrel of a pistol held in Cord's hand. He saw Cord's grinning face and heard, "Now, how 'bout you getting yourself up and outta here very quietly and go hide yourself somewhere, because if I see you on the street, I might be tempted to kill you. Understand?"

The man struggled to his feet, glanced to the woman and back to Cord, "You just made a big mistake, do you know who I am?"

"No, all I know is you are a rude, ill-mannered, big lummox that picks on women!"

"You ain't heard the last o' this!" he growled.

"If you want to stay healthy and keep enough teeth in your mouth to eat, it better be the last!" threatened Cord, still holding the pistol on the man. "Now git!" he ordered, waving the pistol to the door.

The man growled, sneered at the woman, and stomped out of the dining room. Most of the other diners applauded and cheered as he left, forcing a grin on Cord's face as he looked at the woman, "Are you all right, ma'am?"

"Yes, thank you." She extended her hand to Cord, and said, "I am Ida Mae Lyst, and you are?"

"I am Cordell Beckett, most folks just call me

Cord," answered Cord as he accepted her hand and gave a cursory shake as he doffed his hat. "And if you'll excuse me, ma'am, I think they're looking for my order," he nodded to the table and the young woman who stood waiting.

Ida Mae smiled, motioned to the chair opposite her and asked, "Won't you join me, Mr. Beckett?"

"You sure ma'am, you don't even know me?"

"I know enough to know you are a gallant gentleman, and that's more than I can say for most men in these parts. Please," motioning to the chair again.

Cord nodded, signaled to the waitress and pulled out the chair to be seated. He placed his hat on the empty chair to his right and as the waitress came near, he asked, "What do you recommend?" with a smile and a nod.

"The steaks are always good, and the beef stroganoff is well received," started the waitress, as she looked to Cord.

Cord nodded, "A steak, medium rare, and all the trimmin's, please," stated Cord.

The waitress nodded, smiled and quickly retreated to the kitchen.

Ida Mae waited until the waitress entered the kitchen then turned to Cord, "Aren't you going to ask me what that was all about?"

"That's your business ma'am, none of my affair."

"But I'm afraid by your *involvement* they will consider it now your affair, as you put it."

"And who are *they?*"

"They like to call themselves the vigilante committee, but what they really are is a bunch of thugs and thieves. What happened, Mr. Beckett, was..." she paused as the waitress returned with his order, setting it before him and backing away.

Cord smiled, savoring the smells of the fresh broiled steak and the potatoes, onions and carrots, the fresh baked rolls and more. He smiled as he lowered his head for a quick prayer of thanks, lifted his face in a smile and reached for the utensils, "You were saying, ma'am?"

"I am surprised, Mr. Beckett, you are not only brave enough to confront the town bully, but you also actually bowed your head in prayer in public! I've seldom seen the like."

"Which, the bully or the prayer?" asked Cord, smiling as he started eating.

The woman lifted her eyebrows, letting a slow smile paint her face and said, "As I was saying before..." and continued her story.

4

CONFRONTATION

"A LITTLE OVER TWO YEARS AGO, MY HUSBAND, CALVIN, came out here from our home in Illinois. He had heard about all the gold strikes and since our farm had suffered from a long drought, he thought that would be the only way to make it. So, he learned a little about gold, came out to Central City and Black Hawk, found most everything already taken, heard about this area and came here. He was fortunate to get a good claim, and in a short time, he struck gold. It was a placer claim, but paid well, and he sent for me. He built a log cabin back in the trees, made a home for us, and sent me the money to come out. When I arrived, I found he had been killed in what they called an accident, but I found out later it was claim jumpers. But I had all the paperwork and tried to get them removed from the claim, but the *Vigilante Committee* were part of the bunch that took over the claim. That man," nodding to the door where the big man disappeared, "is their bully-boy and he was supposed to get me out of town. I guess the idea of killing a woman was more than they wanted to fight; it's all right to kill a man, but a woman..." she shrugged.

Cord nodded his understanding, kept eating and waited for more.

"So, I don't know what to do now. Are you staying around town long?"

Cord ignored her question as he asked, "If you did gain possession of the claim, then what? Surely you could not work it."

"Oh but I could. I know as much about gold panning and sluicing as anyone; it's not that complicated."

"And you would get down and dirty to do that?" asked Cord, chuckling.

"Yes, I would. I do have my pride, but given the lack of choices as to what a respectable woman can do in this town, well...down and dirty does not sound so bad."

Cord grinned, "And this vigilante committee, do you know who all is involved?"

"There is a man who calls himself Jerry Malcolm who leads them, but there are at least a dozen others involved with him."

Cord had been finishing his meal and the piece of pie for desert when he heard the name. It stopped him as he brought the fork to his mouth, and he looked at the woman, "Are you sure about that name?"

"Yes, why?"

"There was a Jerry Malcolm that was part of the Jayhawkers back in Missouri, during and after the war."

"That's probably the same man. I have heard talk that some people say they were Red Legs, because they act much the same. They think the law, what little there is, does not apply to them and they consider themselves the law, that's why they say they are vigilantes." She paused, leaned forward, frowning, "How do you know about this Jerry Malcolm being a part of the Jayhawkers?"

Cord dropped his eyes and leaned back, leaving the fork on the plate with the last of the pie, folded his hands across his chest, "That's where I'm from - Missouri."

Cord reached for the cup and holding his coffee close as he looked at the woman seated across from him. "Are you certain your husband properly filed the claim?"

"Yes. I have the papers in my room and they were filed with the Griffith Mining District and he also filed them with the county seat, which was in Idaho Springs at the time. He also showed he had proven up on the claim with his work and investments. But..." she sighed heavily, "those men try to say it was abandoned. But it wasn't!" she pleaded, leaning forward. "He built a cabin on the claim and his things were there and as soon as I came out, I moved into the cabin, but that's when they came and loaded up everything and threw me in a wagon and hauled everything, me included, into town here and ordered me to leave."

"When was this?" asked Cord.

"Two days ago! And I don't have the money to pay my fare back to Illinois even if I wanted to go, but I don't!" she firmly affirmed, leaning on the edge of the table and looking at Cord.

Cord reached into his vest pocket, withdrew his pocket watch and looked to see the time. It was closing in on two in the afternoon, and he replaced the watch, looked at Ida Mae and asked, "Are you sure you want to go back to the cabin, take back the claim? It will be hard work and you'll need to be able to defend yourself."

"Yes! I have a Colt Pocket Revolver," she began as she glanced around and reached into her reticule and withdrew the pocket-sized pistol to show Cord. "And I will get whatever you might think I need."

————

CORD RENTED a wagon and team at the livery and rode into the town to meet Ida Mae at the General Store on Main Street. They walked in together and they began gathering the necessities of tools, foodstuffs, and other items, stacking them on the counter. Cord looked at the rack of rifles behind the counter, pointed to a coach gun shotgun and asked to see it. The clerk looked at Cord, glanced to the woman and with raised eyebrows, took the gun from the rack and lay it on the counter. Cord handed it to Ida, "Hold this," and nodded to the gun.

Ida accepted the shotgun, right hand wrapped around the pistol grip, left hand under the forestock, and Cord grinned, "Good, good." He turned to the clerk, "We'll take three boxes of shells for the coach gun, and that Winchester," pointing to a rifle on the rack, "and three boxes of .44's for that. Then give us a tally so we can load up."

As they were seated on the wagon, Cord handed Ida Mae the shotgun, and showed her how to break the action and load the shells into the two barrels and snap it shut. "Now, keep that thing on your lap and pointed away from me. It won't fire until you cock the hammers, so most folks keep their thumbs on the hammers so they're ready to use it." He glanced down to Ida Mae's hand as she lay her thumb across the hammers and put her finger on the trigger guard, smiling at Cord.

He chuckled as he reached for the lines for the team, glanced to the boardwalk across the street and saw the previously encountered bully leaning against the porch post of the assay office and scowling at Cord and Ida. Cord spoke softly to Ida, "Your friend over there does not look too happy," and slapped the reins to the butts of the team and started from town.

"I'm sure he'll run and tell Jerry Malcolm and the others about what he saw."

Cord grinned, "I haven't had anybody tattlin' on me since I was in the schoolhouse."

"So, how long do you plan on staying on in Georgetown?" asked Ida.

"Oh, long enough. I'm not putting down roots or anything like that, but...long enough."

The wagon road, such as it was, sided Clear Creek as they left the town behind and traveled upstream with granite-tipped peaks casting their long afternoon shadows across the narrow-bottomed valley. With steep sided rocky mountains rising on both sides of the creek and road, the cool air wafted from the north, climbing up their backs and pushing them onward. It was just a little more than a mile and a half from town where Ida pointed out the claim and the cabin. It appeared abandoned, the remains of a sluice box cocked at an awkward angle at the edge of the creek, piles of worked rock and gravel stacked beside the creek bed, and the chuckling clear waters of the creek splashing over the rocky bottom, gave the place a sense of foreboding, death even. Ida touched Cord's arm, pointing to the rockpiles, "I found my husband's body there, beside the sluice box."

Cord nodded, turned the team to cross the shallow creek and move to the tree line beside the cabin. Even the cabin had been vandalized, the lone window broken, the door hanging askew on the leather hinges. Inside the small table leaned on three legs, the two chairs kicked aside, the bed at the back had been claimed by a racoon who reared back, hissed, and pawed at the air, before scampering past Cord and out the door. Ida said, "I'll start cleaning if you'll unload the wagon."

"How 'bout we fix the shelves," nodding to the broken shelves over the counter, "and whatever else needs fixin' 'fore we unload. It won't take long."

Ida forced a smile, nodded, and went to the wagon to retrieve her bag and take it behind the cabin, calling over her shoulder, "I'm gonna get into some work clothes!"

————

AND WORK THEY DID. While Ida started in the cabin, Cord checked the claim stakes and markers, replaced those that had been removed or destroyed, and noticed someone had tried to re-stake the claim with bogus markers, which he removed. By the time dusk lowered its curtain, the cabin was clean, stocked, and ready for living. The small stove was sufficient to warm the cabin and to cook on and Ida had a pot of stew lifting its tantalizing aroma into the small cabin and making it feel like a home. Two lanterns were lit, one hanging near the cookstove, the other sitting on the table, now repaired and standing strong. Cord leaned on the table, watching Ida as she puttered about, looking every bit the homemaker. She glanced to Cord, smiled, and said, "Dinner is almost ready!"

Cord chuckled, "I'm going to check on the animals, fetch 'em a little grass, check on that corral again, just have a look-see around." He had returned the wagon and retrieved his horse, mule and dog, and returned to repair the small corral just before dark.

Ida smiled, "That's good. We've had a couple riders pass by that were craning their necks to look at what we were doing, so, I reckon word has gotten back to the vigilance committee. We can expect a visit from them at any time."

"Well, I showed you how to use that coach gun and the Winchester. You handled 'em both better'n most men, so I don't think you have anything to worry about."

Ida frowned, "You're not leaving, are you?"

Cord grinned, "No, but I'll roll my blankets in the trees, just to be safe. 'Sides, folks might talk if'n I was to stay here in the cabin, you know."

"Oh, I don't think talk is the thing I need to be worryin' about," Ida laughed, turning back to her stew.

5

CLAIM

A LOW GROWL CAME FROM BLUE JUST AS CORD CAME awake. He lay still, moving only his eyes as he searched the layout of the claim and the cabin from his hidden camp just inside the trees. His position was a bit higher on the slope of the mountain and offered him a view of the entire layout. He spotted three riders coming from the road, moving slowly and as quietly as possible, but horses hooves, shoes, and rocky terrain do not make for silence. Cord came from his blankets, slipped his pistol into his holster, grabbed up his Winchester and with the dark shadows masking his movements, worked his way to the edge of the trees, and behind the cabin. He moved around the side of the cabin, looking between the log ends to see the three stepping down from their horses. They stood together with the man in the center giving orders and motioning toward the cabin. He reached behind his cantle and brought out what Cord instantly recognized as torches, sizeable sticks wrapped with cloth that was probably soaked in kerosene. The leader was fumbling in his shirt pocket as Cord stepped from the corner of the cabin, rifle at his hip and spoke, "I wouldn't do that, you might burn yourself!"

The three turned, the leader frozen in place, holding the unlit torches. The other two grabbing for pistols, but Cord's Winchester bucked and roared, stabbing the darkness with flame as he fired, jacked another round and fired again, taking both men down, one with a bullet that split his breastbone, the other with a bullet in his hip. One was dead, the other whimpering on the ground as the man in the middle growled, "You just bought yourself a trip to the graveyard, buster!"

"Oh? I'm not the one that's staring down the muzzle of a Winchester! You ready to join your friends?" asked Cord as he jacked another round into the chamber of his rifle, the clatter of the lever loud in the darkness. He heard the door slowly open behind him and spoke over his shoulder, "Sorry 'bout wakin' you up, ma'am, but we have some visitors I thought you might wanna meet."

He heard the hammers on the coach gun lock back as Ida stepped beside him. "Oh? Isn't it an odd hour for visitors? I mean, it's dark out."

"Ummhmm, but they came with their own lights and that'n," motioning with the muzzle of his

Winchester, "was just gettin' ready to light 'em when I discouraged him."

"Maybe he should leave and take his trash with him, don't you think?" asked Ida, holding the coach gun with its muzzle showing black holes at the visitor.

"Or, we could use their bodies to fill in the prospect holes your husband dug."

"Nah, I think they'd get to stinkin' and ruin everything with their smell."

"Maybe you're right," answered Cord, chuckling and enjoying the nervous dance the torch holder was doing as he watched and listened. Cord scowled at the man, "Now, drop them torches, get your friends on their horses and get gone!"

"But, but, that'ns dead," whined the man, pointing to the body of the dead man with now empty hands, "an' that'ns hurt an' bleedin', prob'ly won't make it back to town."

"Then I reckon you better hurry up, cuz if we start buryin', we'll be diggin' three graves! Oh, and be sure to tell your boss who dunnit. Tell him it's the same man that ran him outta Oro City!"

Cord chuckled as the man rode away, moonlight showing the two trailed horses, one with a man tied into the saddle, the other draped over his saddle. He looked at Ida Mae, who frowned as she looked at Cord, "Ran him out of Oro City?"

Cord grinned, nodded, looked at the moon that was waning from full, "It's late. We better try to get some sleep. Daylight comes mighty early in these mountains!" He turned away and started back to his bedroll in the trees as Ida Mae stepped up into her cabin, shaking her head at the mystery of the man who had been helping her.

She was up early and preparing breakfast by the light of the lanterns, wondering all the while what the next few days would bring. She hummed as she mixed the batter for flapjacks, heard a light knock on the door and called out, "If you're Cord, come on in! Breakfast is almost ready."

The door pushed open and Cord's smiling face pushed into the light, glancing about the interior of the cabin before he stepped inside. He hung his hat on the peg beside the door, walked to the table and sat down, watching Ida Mae puttering about with her fixing. He chuckled to himself, enjoying the look and smells of a home cooked breakfast. He remembered his mother doing much the same, humming as she worked, always smiling, always happy. But the remembrance of home and family stirred other emotions, anger, frustration, sadness and loss. He shook his head, trying to clear his mind of the past and looked at Ida Mae. She was an attractive woman, not what some men would call beautiful, but pretty and wholesome. She had a good figure, filling out her work britches better than any man or any woman he had ever seen in such attire, which was only some of

the native women in their buckskin tunics and
leggings. He grinned at the thought, but even that
image brought painful memories; the memory of
Yellow Singing Bird, the Mouche Ute woman that
had traveled with him and chose to stay with him.
The woman he had considered making his life partner, until another attack by the former Jayhawkers
killed her and wounded him. *Why is it that every good
memory is saddled by sadness and death?*

He shook his head to clear his thoughts just as
Ida Mae sat a plate full of flapjacks and bacon before
him. "There's fresh butter in the bowl, and some
maple syrup in the jar," she said, smiling and pointing. Cord nodded, smiled, and bowed his head and
said a silent prayer of thanksgiving, and lifted his
eyes as he reached for the butter and more.

Ida filled her own plate, sat it opposite Cord and
seated herself. "I like a man that is thankful and
thoughtful. I've seen few men that had the courage
to show their faith before others. It's refreshing." Ida
smiled as she started pouring syrup on the flapjacks.

Cord said, "It's a struggle with me. There's too
many bad memories and arguments I've had with
the Lord, and it's not easy to turn from those
thoughts to good thoughts and thanksgiving in
prayer. My father was a preacher and..." he shrugged
and used the fork to cut a big bite of flapjacks.

They ate in silence until Ida rose to fetch the
coffee pot and refill their cups. As she poured his full,
she looked at him and asked, "So, what now?"

"I reckon that'll be up to them. They might try to come in force sometime today, prob'ly about mid-day, their kind are not usually early risers," he chuckled. "Then we'll see how we stand up to 'em and what they decide to do. They have what some might call mob authority, because they have the numbers and the guns and the will to use them, they think they can do whatever they want. Georgetown is still young and without official law, so they will run over anybody that gets in their way, until..." he shrugged.

"Until?"

"Until somebody stands up to them. Usually when that happens, others find their nerve and join with the good people and the outlaws usually move on to easier pickins."

"Do you think that will happen here?"

Cord grinned, took a sip of his coffee as he pushed his plate aside, "We'll just do what we can to *make* it happen here."

While Ida Mae tended to household tasks, Cord began preparing for an attack. He snaked a couple logs from the trees to stack off the corner of the cabin, but with a whipsaw lying atop the logs, they appeared to be preparations for other things. A cluster of rocks sided a big boulder at the edge of the trees on the opposite side of the cabin, and he dug a slight hole behind a pile of diggings that sat on the near bank of the creek, a pile apparently already mined by Ida's husband. The lone window in the cabin had been broken out and the shutter hung on leather hinges. Cord repaired the shutters that had a slit for a firing hole on the low side. He repaired the door, new thicker leather hinges and drop bar on the inside. He stood back, looking at the preparations, and satisfied, stepped inside to see a smiling Ida Mae ready to come out. She said, "Well, you've been busy!"

"Ummhmm, and here's what we need to do..." he began as he started outlining their defense strategy. He had placed his coach gun behind the logs, his Spencer behind the rocks, and his Winchester would be in his hands. He had his Colt in the holster at his hip, but it was hidden by his long duster. He directed Ida how to use the coach gun and the firing port at the shutters, "But keep your Winchester within reach. They might get past me and try to storm the door. From within, your rifle will be just as deadly shooting through the door as not, so don't be afraid to use it. If they're storming the door, they aren't doing it to bring you a bouquet of flowers!"

She smiled, nodded and started to say something, but the clatter of hooves on the hard-packed road told of the arrival of more than one rider or prospector. Cord nodded, stepped outside, and pulled the door closed behind him.

6

FACE-OFF

As Cord stepped outside, he took his marshal badge from his pocket and pinned it on his vest, pulled his duster over the top of it. He did not want to show the badge unless absolutely necessary; he had found it easier to move about and find out about happenings without a badge. Folks were a bit more talkative when there is no special authority nearby. Cord let a bit of a grin split his face as he stood before the cabin, watching the group of five men come thundering up the wagon road, raising a lot more dust and making more noise than necessary, but Cord knew that was the way of a gang; the noise and such helped bolster their courage and bravado. He saw the group was led by the bully from town, the big man making his horse appear small and his glowering stare shaped into a snarl as his anger began to build. He jerked the reins on his mount to the side, almost making the animal stumble but the horse gained his footing as the bunch dropped from the road and splashed into the creek.

As they came from the water, they started to spread out, but Cord barked at them as he lifted his rifle, "Don't do it! You men best stay behind the big boy, less'n you want to be weighted down with enough lead that would make you sink in the creek!"

They reined up, some leaning to the side to see who was barking orders and heard the big boy say, "Spead out like I said!"

One man jerked hard on the reins of his horse, leaning to his left and starting to move away from the others, but the blast from the Winchester in Cord's hands startled them all and when the bullet ripped into the pommel of the man's saddle and tore into his hip, he screamed, and grabbed at his hip. He looked up at Cord and to the big man, "He shot me!"

The big man growled, "Take him!" and the men grabbed for their holstered pistols, jerking the heads of their horses to the side, each trying to get sight of Cord, but Cord dove behind the logs, came up with his coach gun and let loose with both barrels that were loaded with double ought buckshot. The men were near enough that only two, the big man known as Jonas Bright and the man beside him, the weasel that had come at them the night before, were hit. Both men were driven back by the blast, and the weasel, Otto Fisher, dropped from his saddle, both hands grabbing at his belly.

Jonas Bright was bloodied across his broad front,

his shirt and vest ripped to shreds, his whiskered chin showing red, as he had one big paw holding his guts inside as he looked with wide eyes showing shock at Cord. "You shot me!" he whimpered, and slid from his saddle.

Cord had dropped behind the logs, quickly reloading the coach gun, as a blast came from the shuttered window and he looked up to see two men on the far side take the brunt of the blast. They were farther away and the buckshot pattern spread wider, bloodying the neck of one of the horses, and blossoming red on two men, but both kept to their saddles, trying to rein the horses around to escape. One man slumped in his saddle, the other struggled to stay aboard, and the last man that had been directly behind Jonas Bright was splashing back through the creek to make his getaway.

Cord snatched up the rifle, shot at a big rock in front of the fleeing outlaw and the whining ricochet stopped him. He turned to look back as Cord said, "Hold it right there!" The man stopped, lifting his free hand and facing Cord as Cord said, "C'mon back. I want you to take a message to your boss! C'mon, I won't shoot."

The man reined his mount around, walked him back through the creek and looking at his fellow outlaws scattered on the ground and bloody, he looked up at Cord. "You didn't give us a chance!" he whined.

"Oh, and I s'pose you five men attacking one man and a woman were here to *give us a chance?*"

"Well...we'd at least talked 'fore we started shootin'."

"I heard your talkin', it was the big boy there that told you to spread out and take us! Now..." started Cord, "the woman there," nodding to the cabin, "is gonna come out with her shotgun, and you'n me are gonna load up these outlaws, and you're takin' 'em back to your boss, Mr. Jerry Malcolm. So, c'mon, let's get it done!"

As they worked loading the bodies, the outlaw, Milo Farwell, said, "You don't know what you done. Malcolm ain't gonna be happy 'bout this. The best thing you can do is pack up an' get out 'fore he comes here his own self. After all, we're the vigilantes and we're the law 'roun'chere."

Cord chuckled, finished loading the last body and tied it down, then turned and casually pulled back his duster to show the marshal's badge as he looked at the wounded man. He was the one that had taken the first bullet that struck his pommel and cut into his hip. He was whimpering and struggling to get his foot in the stirrup when he looked up to see the badge. He froze in place, his eyes grew wide and he almost whispered, "You're a federal marshal?"

Cord nodded, gave the man a hand up and handed him the leads to the four horses that carried their bloody carcasses. He stepped back as the man nudged his mount to cross the creek. After he crossed and the last of the led horses crossed, the man looked back, shook his head and hollered, "I ain't talkin' to Malcolm, I'm getting' outta here!"

Cord nodded, waved, and turned back to the cabin. Ida looked at him and said, "What prompted that?"

"Oh, I reckon he had a sudden inspiration to do right," chuckled Cord, "You got any o' that coffee left?"

Ida Mae nodded, smiled and turned back to the cabin. "I sure am glad you had those men haul off their garbage. It would get to stinkin' after a while."

————

As MILO LED the four horses into town, the bloody sight drew a crowd and folks hollered, "Who dunnit?"

At first, Milo was hesitant to say, but the more people asked, he finally answered, "It were a federal marshal, back up the crick a ways. Him an' that woman in the cabin, they done it!" he growled, mad at both the marshal and himself for what happened. He reined up in front of the Big Nugget saloon and stepped down. The noisy crowd had drawn the attention from those inside and the rest of the vigilantes stepped out on the boardwalk to see the sight of their fellow vigilantes draped over their horses backs. The watching men mumbled among themselves, asking questions of Milo that went unanswered as he stepped down, slapped the reins of his mount and those of the other horses around the hitchrail. He looked up at the others, showed his bloody hip and side, "Where's the doc?"

"Down to his office, where else?" snapped one of the men that stood before the saloon.

"I'm goin' down there. Gotta get patched up!"

"You better talk to Malcolm first!" declared one man.

Milo waved him off, struggled to step up to the boardwalk, then turned away and started off toward the doctor's office. The other vigilantes looked at the four bodies, one man lifting each head and calling out the names of the dead, looked at their wounds, then moved to the next man. When he came to the last man, the big man called Jonas Bright, he shook his head, "I din't think anything could kill this big lummox!"

When Jerry Malcolm pushed his way through the gathered men, they willingly gave way and watched as he looked at the bodies. He glanced to the others, "Where's the other'n? I sent five men!"

"The other'n was Milo Farwell. He was wounded and went to the doctor to get patched up, he was pretty bloody."

Malcolm showed his disgust and anger and he turned on his heel to go back into the saloon. He barked over his shoulder, "Tell him to come in as soon as he gets back!"

The man called Malcolm prided himself in his

appearance. He wore a black frock coat over a brocade vest that showed black and silver. His gambler striped trousers were charcoal grey with a thin stripe to accent. He kept his boots with a high shine, and his black pistol belt and holster were mounted with silver and held a silver mounted engraved Colt Navy with carved ivory grips. His black flat crowned hat had a silver mounted band, and the man's black hair hung to his collar. There had been another one of the Red Legs that prided himself in his appearance much like Malcolm, the one called Dave Poole that had been killed trying to rob a stage coming from Canon City.

Jerry Malcolm pushed his way past the others and went to the office that was to the far side of the bar and behind closed doors. He pushed his way inside, doffed his hat and hung it on the rack, dropped into the chair behind the desk and sat with arms on the desktop, his head hanging. *What was it that Milo said last night - that the man that chased me out of Oro City was coming after me? But... who was that? Wait, it was that man on the grulla that wore the duster, he's the one that shot Dave Poole and some of the others. He's the one that scared Newt into leaving and the rest of us left with him. Surely it's not him. How would he know I was here?"*

He looked around, glanced to his safe that held the papers of the claims his men had taken, and the stolen pokes. He had several thousand dollars' worth of dust in there. He could load them into a pair of saddle bags and leave all this behind. That would be more than enough to give him a good start anywhere. *Yeah, I'll wait till after dark, then out the back door!* He chuckled to himself, and like most outlaws, thought himself smarter than any other. *I'll send the rest of the men back after that man and Lyst's widow, and I'll be long gone when they get back!* He chuckled to himself as he relaxed and leaned back in his chair to wait for Milo to come in and give his report.

7

CONFLICT

"You shoulda heard the shootin' up Clear Creek way yestiddy! I'm tellin' ya, sounded like I was back in the war!" declared the man leaning against the bar at the Lucky Lady, as he grabbed his drink and quaffed it down, wiped his lips and nodded to the barkeep for another.

"I heard about it, but what was it all about?" asked a sourdough looking older man with a full face of whiskers.

"It was down to the claim that fella Lyst had 'fore them vigilantes came. I rode down there after, but weren't nothin' happenin', but it looked like some-body's livin' in his cabin. Mebbe that's what it was all about."

"You know, there was a ruckus down by the Big Nugget saloon, seems one of 'em brought in four horses with four bodies strapped on, an' that fella Malcolm was none too happy!"

"Ain't he the one what bosses them vigilantes?"

"Ummhmm, an' the way folks was talkin', them dead ones were all vigilantes!"

"Sounds like trouble's comin', we better have another drink!" proclaimed the first man, waving over the barkeep for refills.

Three men had been sitting at a nearby table and listened to the conversation until one spoke up, "There was another shootin' durin' the other night. Two were killed, another'n brought 'em in, and it happened at the same claim."

Everyone looked around, and talk began to flow. The speaker at the table stood, lifted his hands and said, "Men, we've been puttin' up with this for too long. We all know who's been doin' it and each of us have been hopin' we could get our pokes full 'fore it happened to us. But the only way it's gonna stop, is if we find out who that was doin' all the shootin' and maybe get on his side for a change!"

The talk among the men rose as several were nodding their agreement and chiming in with their thoughts until a man slammed the swinging doors as he rushed in, shoutin', "Hey! They're sayin' that Malcolm ran out! They said he left in the middle of the night, after he lost so many of his men. Some was sayin' he was runnin' scared! That fella what done the shootin' sent a message back to Malcolm sayin' he was the one what drove him outta Oro City and he was comin' after Malcolm!"

The roar of the crowd raised and drinks were

flowing as they bellied up to the bar and added their thoughts to the conversation. The man who had been at the table and raised his voice, now stood at the bar and raised his hands for quiet, as he started, "Men! Men! Listen!" Most of the others quieted and turned to face the man called Moses Wynkoop. "I don't know if it's over, but I heard that the one called Milo Farwell said that man said he was a Federal Marshal, that was before Milo mounted up and left town, before tellin' that to the rest of the vigilantes. So, I'm thinkin' we need to find that marshal, see if we can get things settled for certain around here, and if not, we should get that sorry excuse for a sheriff over in Idaho Springs to come down here to the new county seat like he's supposed to, if not, we need to get us a new sheriff!"

"Hear, hear!" declared one of the others at the bar and the call was echoed by the crowd. Then the talk began about making the speaker, Moses Wynkoop, their new sheriff. One man grinned, "And besides, that widow woman is kinda purty. I think Moses there already knows that!"

Wynkoop added, "So, who wants to come with me to that claim and talk to the shooter?"

Several men answered and the crowd started for the door, led by Moses Wynkoop.

THE TRAIL from town to the claim was well traveled, but still a narrow road barely suitable for a wagon, and Cord did not want to wait for another attack at the cabin. "They have to come from town, and there's only one road, so..."

"What are you saying?"

"My dad said he learned during his time in uniform that the man that is only defending is at a disadvantage and his attacker can decide when and how the fight will start. He said it's always better to take the initiative - decide when and where you want to fight. It's always best to be on the offense than defense," answered Cord as he slipped the Spencer in the scabbard. The Winchester was in the scabbard under his right leg, the Spencer on the opposite side. The coach gun was tied down behind the cantle and he had found some canisters of black powder and some twisted fuses that he might find useful.

"Don't you want me to come? I think I did all right with the shotgun last time!" said a smiling Ida Mae.

"Yes you did. So it might be best for you to stay here at the claim, just in case they get around me and still come here."

"Oh, but how can they get around you? There is no other way to get here from town."

"Ummhmm, but..." he shrugged and her eyes flared as she realized what he was implying.

————

"I THOUGHT Malcolm told Milo to come back to the tavern after he got doctored up; what'd he do?" asked one of the vigilantes known as Boston who always wore a dirty derby and was seated at a table in the Big Nugget.

"He did, but last I saw, Milo was headin' outta town and in a mighty big hurry!" answered the man called Chapo across the table from him as he was lifting his mug to his lips. He was a dark skinned Mexican and no one knew his real name.

"Does Malcolm know that?"

"I dunno, you wanna tell him?"

"Hah!" snorted a third man known as Gooseneck because of his thin frame and long neck. "Last time somebody tried to tell Malcolm sumpin', he ended up on the floor in his own blood!"

"It's been kinda quiet in there. He's usually got him a woman, but the light's been out an' he ain't come out," said Boston, glancing to the door.

"Wal, he tol' Yaqui to get the rest of us together and go get that guy at the claim. He also said if we don't do it, and that guy doesn't kill us all, he'd finish the job himself! And I don' know 'bout'chu, but I'm more 'fraid of that Mex Yaqui than I am of Malcolm!" declared Gooseneck.

"What'chu mean he'd finish the job, you mean he'd actually get outta his office and get his hands dirty?"

"No, I think he meant if that fella at the claim din't kill us, an' we failed, that he'd kill us!"

The men leaned in on the table, lowered their voices, and Boston said, "Look, there's only six of us left, an' he already done in the first three, and the last bunch had five an' he kilt four, so, I'm thinkin' our chances ain't none too good!"

"Yeah, but how we gonna get out of it?" asked Chapo.

"We could always leave, tonight, 'fore daylight when Yaqui will be lookin' for us."

"No, no, señor, Yaqui is more Indian than Mex and he will know if you try to leave. I'll take my chances with the man at the claim, not Yaqui!"

————

YAQUI WAS a suspicious man as were most men of outlaw ways. None were willing to trust others because they know they are untrustworthy themselves, and if they would be willing to shoot down a friend for cause, so would others. After he received his orders from Malcolm, the tall man with the short jacket and typical attire of the Mexican gaucho, walked through the darkness to the livery. He knew Malcolm took pride in his big black gelding with Andalusian traits, and would never leave without his prized horse. If the horse was still in the livery, Malcolm would still be in his office or his room. And the big black was there, tossing his head in greeting when Yaqui stepped into the dark livery, the big door standing open to let the first light of day show the interior. Satisfied, Yaqui went to the stall of his horse, the big dapple-grey gelding, and began saddling the spirited animal. He had a job to do and he was anxious to put it behind him, for he had other plans for his future and those plans did not include Jerry Malcolm.

8

ELECTION

Cord remembered a sizable rocky escarpment at the edge of a talus slope on the north side of the road. No more than forty feet above the road, the shoulder of basaltic rock offered the overlook he needed. He tethered the animals in the trees on the shoulder and climbed to the rocks, the Spencer on a sling at his back, the canister of black powder in the bag on his shoulder. The first light of early morning cast long shadows as the sun bent its long rays over the mountain that had taken the name of the first men who found gold in the valley, Griffith Mountain. Cord moved a couple rough edged rocks out of the way, making a place for him to have both a seat and cover and rest for his rifle. From his vantage point, he could see to the bend in the road that came from Georgetown, about a half mile as the road sided Clear Creek and bent back to the north around the steep-shouldered mountain. With everything in place, now came the wait, and Cord's mind, always active, began to take him down the trail of memories.

His mother, Narcissa, stood at the counter, humming as she prepared the meal, always with a smile on her face, and his dad, Charles or Chuck, walked softly up behind her, slipping his hands around her waist and resting his chin on her shoulder, so he could whisper intimate secrets into her ear. Both were grinning and his mother nudged the cheek of his father, and he moved away, smiling broadly and satisfied with their exchange. He glanced to Cord, "Someday you'll understand," chuckled and pulled the chair back so he could take his place at the head of the table. On one side of the setting, lay his well-worn Bible, on the other, the recent copy of the Kansas City Journal-Post newspaper. He opened the paper and began to read.

Cord looked at his younger sister, Marybel, the blonde-haired mischief maker, and his younger brother, Charles, who was busy with a wooden puzzle, frowning as he worked. It was a placid scene, and the last image he had of his family together. After the breakfast, Cord would go to his favorite spot in the trees and his lofty retreat, to read his newest book, *Bucaniers of America,* an exciting account of the buccaneers and pirates of the Caribbean. While he sat in his favorite Sycamore tree, he heard the alarming sounds of gunshots that he would later find were the sounds of the attack by Red Legs that destroyed his family and his farm and would set him on this journey of retribution. And the only known member of that gang that was in this country was the one called Jerry Malcolm.

The rattle of hooves on the hard-packed road brought Cord from his reverie. He lifted his binoculars and searched the valley, and the rising dust told of the bunch that was coming up the road. He narrowed his view and saw figures that were unfamiliar, but their attire and attitudes told Cord these were more of the vigilantes. He lowered the binoculars, pulled the canister of black powder close and unwrapped the twisted fuse. With another glance to the riders, he dug out a lucifer and struck the match, lit the fuse and ensured it was burning, he cocked his arm back, and lofted the canister in a long arch toward the roadway. Just before the canister landed, it exploded in a black ball of smoke and flame, the roaring blast reverberated across the canyon, the echo bouncing from side to side, seeming to amplify with the blast.

The sudden explosion startled the horses and all six animals jerked, jumped, and began bucking, trying to unseat their riders. With heads down between their front feet, the reins were jerked from some of the riders, others were pulled forward, all were shouting and cursing, but every man had all he could do to try to bring his mount to a stop. Cord watched as the man with the sombrero, who appeared to be the leader, gained control of his mount, stopped, watching the others and looking

around for the source of the blast and glared at
Cord as he stood behind the rocks, rifle in hand.
Cord hollered, "You fellas best go back and tell
Malcolm it's all over! Any of you try to go any
further up this road will be riding into your own
grave!"

The man known as Yaqui leaned forward on the
big flat saddle horn of his Mexican saddle and said,
"Who are you, an' why should we do what you say?"

"I'm the one that sent your friends back, tied
over their saddles. Now, I don't want to have to
burden you with the same task, but I'm ready and
before you can clear leather, this .56 Spencer will
send you a more personal message that you might
understand a little better!" The men that sat their
horses before Cord were only slightly familiar, maybe
he had seen them in town, but they were not part of
the original Red Legs.

Yaqui started to move, but the rattle of hooves
from behind him made him turn and he recognized
one of his men that had been left behind at the
tavern. It was the lanky one known as Gooseneck
and he was waving and shouting. When he came
near, he hollered to Yaqui, "Hey! Thot you oughta
know! Malcolm skipped town! He left on the early
stage, emptied his safe and office, left his horse
behind and he's gone!"

Cord chuckled, and called out, "Now ain't that
interestin'? Your boss sent you to attack us, and he
took off while you were gone! Just like him, that's

what he did in Oro City and other places all the way back to Missouri!"

Cord heard other riders coming and looked down the road to see a group of about a dozen men coming up the road behind the vigilantes. He heard the skinny rider beside the leader say, "Them's some fellas from the Lucky Lady, they were talkin' 'bout gettin' 'em a lawman, a sheriff or sumpin'."

The leader known as Yaqui looked from Goose-neck to the approaching riders, glanced back at Cord and tipped his sombrero, "Maybe some other time, señor?" and turned away, nudged his mount past the others and started back to town. The rest of his bunch followed, and as they passed the townsfolk, there were occasional nods, no exchanged greetings, and the last of the vigilantes rode from the valley of Georgetown.

Cord returned to his tethered mount, loaded his gear and climbed aboard. He nudged Kwitcher to the road after the townspeople passed and out of curios-ity, followed them. He was surprised to see them leave the road and cross the creek below Ida's cabin, but he grinned as he saw her standing in front of the cabin, shotgun in hand, as the men reined up and the leader, Moses Wynkoop, spoke. "Mornin' ma'am. I'm Moses Wynkoop," he motioned to the men with him, "We came to check on you and your man, everything all right?"

"Well, everything seems to be all right, but he's

not *my man*. He's a friend that chose to help me when no one else would."

"Uh, yes'm, we're sorry about that, but..."

"Well, you're right about one thing, you're sorry all right!" she declared, starting to lift the shotgun.

Wynkoop saw her movement, lifted his hand to stay her, and added, "Well, ma'am, we know we as a community have failed to do what's right, but we're determined to do better. Uh, is the man around? We'd like to talk to him if we could."

"There's nothing he can tell you that I can't, besides, he's right there behind you!" she said, grinning and nodding toward Cord who sat on Kwitcher, listening to the exchange.

The men turned to look behind them and saw Cord, his flat brimmed hat turned down, his collar up and looking more like a shadow than anything.

Ida Mae asked, "Why'd you want to talk to him anyway? He has no say about this claim."

Wynkoop turned back to Ida, "It's not about the claim, it's about somethin' we heard." He paused, looking from Ida to Cord who had moved to the side to go past the men and now stepped down from his saddle at the corner of the cabin. Wynkoop looked from Ida to Cord and asked, "May we step down and talk?"

Ida grinned, glanced to Cord, and back to Wynkoop, and answered, "Step down."

Wynkoop moved closer, looked at Cord, "We heard you were a marshal, is that true?" His comment surprised Ida who turned, frowning, to look at Cord for his answer.

Cord asked, "Where'd you hear that?"

"Uh, seems one o' the vigilantes told some folks you were a marshal. But he left town so…" he shrugged.

"And why are you askin'?" inquired Cord, neither admitting nor denying the question.

"Well, we need a lawman. The only sheriff is o'er to Idaho Springs and when we moved the county seat, he refused to leave Idaho Springs. And we don't have any law in Georgetown and we need a good lawman."

"You plannin' on building a jail and everything?"

Wynkoop looked at the others, many were nodding and agreeing, and turned back to Cord, "That's right. We'll get started on it right away."

"Well, I've got other obligations but…" he looked at Wynkoop and asked, "What about you, why can't you be the law? You've led these folks up here and such." He looked at the crowd, "How 'bout it men? Don't you think this fella would make a good sheriff?"

The men looked at Wynkoop, one another, mumbled among themselves, nodding their heads and more and Cord called out, "All right, all in favor of this man," he lowered his voice, and looked at Wynkoop, "what's your name?" when he heard the answer, he continued, "this man, Moses Wynkoop, to be your new sheriff, raise your hand!"

He looked at the group and one after another a hand was raised until all present had their hands in the air. Cord grinned, looked at Wynkoop, "Congratulations! You just won your first election. You're the new sheriff!"

Cord looked at Ida Mae, "You got any coffee on?"

She smiled, nodded, and they went into the cabin as the others mounted up to ride back to Georgetown, and there was considerable talk among the men with a new lighthearted air among them.

9

IDAHO SPRINGS

"Moses said he would be checking on me and my claim as often as he could," said Ida Mae, a timid smile splitting her face. She stood just outside the door of her cabin and the dim light of early morning began to stretch long shadows across the flat of the claim below the cabin. Cord has swung aboard Kwitcher and Blue was looking from Cord to Ida Mae and his wagging tail told of his anxiousness to be on the trail. Cord nodded, "He seems to be a good man, and I think he'll do well. If you get tired of chasin' the rainbow of gold, you might set your cap for that man, might make a good husband for you," chuckled Cord, grinning.

"I'm not thinkin' 'bout that right now. I want to get some dust in my poke 'fore I think of anything else. Thanks to you, I've got my home back and more, so I'll stay busy enough to keep my mind occupied with proper things," she smiled, shading her eyes from the beginning of morning.

"Well, if I'm back this way, I'll stop in," stated Cord, reining Kwitcher toward the creek and the road leading to Georgetown.

"You do that, and if I hear you're in the area and don't stop, I'll come lookin' for you with my shotgun!" she threatened, laughing.

————

THE MOUNTAIN SHADOWS cloaked the settlement of Georgetown as Cord kept to the stage road that sided Clear Creek. The sleepy town had few early risers; he heard a hand pump creaking beyond the row of business buildings, a lazy dog lifted an eyebrow to open one eye as he passed, and somewhere a chicken was bragging about its latest treasure just dropped into its straw nest. Cord grinned as he rode through the town, saw one early riser sweeping off his boardwalk and nodded to Cord who returned the nod as he passed by, but he soon had an unhindered view of the cascading waters of Clear Creek and the quiet road that pointed northeast.

The road bent to the east as it sided a lone steep butte that dropped off where the road merged with another from Empire City. Now facing into the rising sun, Cord kept to the road making his way through the middle of the goldfields that stretched from

below Georgetown, to north of Central City and Black
Hawk. After talking with some of the men from town,
he knew the stage that had been taken by Malcolm
was the route bound for Central City and Black
Hawk, but there was no way of knowing how far
Malcolm would be traveling. Since he was the only
known member of the Red Legs that had attacked his
farm, Cord was determined to find the man and
maybe learn the whereabouts of some of the others.

It was late morning when Cord rode into the
stage stop at Mill City. Although it was no more
than a few log buildings, the Mill City House
appeared to be two cabins that had been joined
together and now served as the stage stop. Cord
reined up, slapped the reins around the hitchrail
and stepped inside the darkened and cool interior. A
matronly woman with an apron and a broad smile
called out, "Welcome stranger, you lookin' for
sumpin' to eat?"

Cord grinned, "I am, what'chu got?"

"Got some fresh elk stew with taters 'n gravy and
lotsa hot coffee!"

"Sounds just like what I need. I'll have some."

Cord had doffed his hat and smiled at the woman
who motioned for him to sit at the table as she
turned away to fetch the fixins. She soon returned
with a smile and both hands full, and with a bit of a
giggle, set the table and sat down across from Cord.
She motioned for him to go ahead and eat and asked,
"Goin' far?"

"Dunno, lookin' for a man, mighta come through here on the stage in the last day or so."

"Don't all the stages stop here now, depends on their timin' an' such. Most go on to Idaho Springs or Georgetown, dependin'. Who ya' lookin' for?"

"Man named Jerry Malcolm. Fancy man, dresses purty with lotsa black and silver, but he's a bad'n."

"Yup, they stopped fer breakfast yestiddy. He was fancy but he was also rude. Thot himself to be sumpin' he ain't! What'cha want with the likes o' him?"

Cord had started eating and had his mouth full when she asked him, and he nodded, reaching for the fresh rolls. He tore open a roll, took a deep breath of the fresh sourdough and smiled and said, "Umm, everything's great! You're a good cook, ma'am."

She smiled, nodding and rose from her seat to return to her stove, soon returning with a big slice of fresh berry pie. She sat it down beside Cord's plate, smiling and nodding and said, "I like to see a man eat, makes me feel good."

After devouring two slices of berry pie, Cord asked, "Berries? What kind of berries are ripe this time o' year?"

"Oh, there's service berries, choke cherries, rasp-berries, and more. I kinda use 'em all," she declared with a broad smile, watching as Cord rose and started to the door. He had lain a dollar coin beside his plate and as he stepped out the door, he said, "I sure thank you for the meal ma'am, I left a little something to say thank you," nodding toward the table.

The woman smiled, "Oh, you din't hafta do that! I just charge all the meals to the stage line and they don't fuss atall."

Cord chuckled and swung aboard Kwitcher, waved Blue to the trail and with a nod and a wave, left the stage stop behind.

It was mid-afternoon when Cord rode into Idaho Springs. The town had been flourishing for some time. Since the war, growth and new discoveries had waned and there were some empty buildings staring with vacant eyes at the road, and the moving of the county seat to Georgetown had not helped the growth of the town. Like most quick blooming towns in the mountains, Idaho Springs had its start with placer mining, and later the lode mining added prosperity. But now, it was not as prosperous as before although it was still a vital town in the area. Cord reined up before the mercantile, stepped down and went inside to look around, and as always, just to listen to any news that folks were anxious to talk about.

"Yessir, that Whale and Crystal mines are still goin' strong an' I think they'll be producin' long after the shine's gone from Central City! After all, we had gold here 'fore them an' we'll still be puttin' it out long after, yessiree." The comments were sounded by one of three men that were gathered around the pot-bellied stove that sat in the corner. A man with a long apron over his ample front was standing near, and noticed Cord enter, left the group and came near, "Yessir, can I help you with sumpin'?"

"Sure, sure. I could use some ammunition for my rifle and shotgun, maybe a box each of twelve-gauge and .44's. And I could use a new shirt, some socks, an'..." Cord paused, looking around and as if as an afterthought, added, "Say, the stage that comes through here an' goes to Black Hawk, which way does it go?"

The clerk grinned, chuckling, "Most folks are just interested in the stage goin' to Denver City, but the one goin' to Black Hawk goes up Virginia Canyon," he pointed toward the back end of the store, "it cuts back to the north at the edge of town, goes up through the mountains yonder."

"And if I was wantin' to stay the night, where'd you recommend?"

"Oh, the Wilson House is just down on the corner, and it's right close to the livery too."

Cord nodded, paid his bill, and turned away. After putting the animals down in the livery and stripping the gear to leave in the storeroom there, he walked to the Wilson House, saddlebags over his shoulder and rifle in hand. He was greeted at the counter, bid welcome, and given a room on the second floor. At the recommendation of the clerk, after cleaning up a mite, he went to the dining room for some supper. After seating himself and placing his order, he looked about, saw no one interesting and chose to look out the window.

His first glimpse out the window showed a man that looked a little familiar, riding a tall bay horse, and leading a high stepping all black gelding with long mane and tail, an unusual look for the western lands. But Cord remembered the talk about the horse left behind by Jerry Malcolm, a horse he had taken great pride in and it was surprising he would be left behind. Then Cord realized where he had seen the man leading the black, he was one of the group that he had accosted on the trail the day before, one of the last of the men that had ridden with Malcolm. Cord watched as the man rode past, but he knew the livery lay in that direction and assumed the man was going to the livery. He resolved to check at the livery after he finished his meal, thinking that wherever that horse was, he might find Malcolm.

10

PURSUIT

Cord was brushing the grulla as he stood in the stall next to the pack mule, taking his time, wanting to be there when the big black gelding was taken. The liveryman had told Cord it was a dark Mexican called Chapo that brought the horse in the night before. "He said he was just stayin' the night, gettin' him somethin' to eat, a place to sleep, and he'd be leavin' early this mornin'. Said he needed to deliver that horse 'fore too long or he wouldn't get paid. Reckon his idee of early and ours ain't quite the same," grumbled the liveryman as he returned to his room at the front of the barn. While most livery stables had a liveryman that was also a farrier and blacksmith, from what Cord could tell, those jobs went unfilled.

The street in front of the livery ran east and west while the building faced to the north and the grey light of early morning began to stretch shadows to

the west before the Mex walked into the livery.
Without speaking to anyone or seemingly pay any
attention to anything, the sleepy-eyed man saddled
his big bay, pulling the latigo tight and tying it off
with a wrap and a tuck. He dropped the stirrup,
grabbed the rein and led the horse from the stall, tied
him off outside the big door and returned for the
black who was showing himself a bit anxious when
he saw the bay taken from his stall. When the Mex
neared, the big gelding tossed his head, showing the
length of his mane and the curve of his neck, he
stepped high, and Cord watched, wondering if the
big horse would try to jump the gate of the stall, but
the Mex held out his hand and said, "*Tranquilo, chico,
tranquilo.*" The gelding reached out his nose for the
man's touch, lowered his head for the halter, and the
man led him from the stall, the big horse high
stepping.

Cord knew the man had looked his way, but Cord
had his back to him as if paying him no mind while
he brushed his grulla. He waited until the man
moved to the door, then started saddling Kwitcher,
rigged the mule, and was soon following the Mex as
he started from the town. Cord had considered just
confronting the man in the livery, but decided to
follow him a spell before any confrontation.

Although Idaho Springs was a sizable settlement,
the streets were dry and dusty and it was easy for
Cord to follow the Mex. With a short jaunt to Second
Street, he turned north, went a block, turned west

and followed the sign that said *Virginia Canyon Road, Central City, Black Hawk.* Cord grinned as he settled back in his saddle, ready for a day's ride through the hills and over the crossing to Central City and Black Hawk. He knew Jerry Malcolm took the stage to Black Hawk, but he did not know what the man had planned, but apparently he had made prior arrangements with Chapo to bring his Andalusian gelding to him, and that had to be a costly move, knowing that Chapo's loyalties were with the Yaqui. Cord had learned a little more about the remainder of Malcolm's gang from Moses Wynkoop, the new sheriff, and was surprised to see any of them still willing to do the bidding of Malcolm, knowing the man had run out on them and taken the stolen gold with him, but Moses thought the rest of the men might try to band together and do something with the stolen claims. "I'm not about to let that happen! We have a good idea where the original claim owners are and what they might want to do, especially now that the gang has been broken up, so..." Moses shrugged, then with a frown, he added, "I am surprised he left that big black gelding behind. Malcolm took great pride in that horse, he liked paradin' up and down the street, showin' him off, getting the attention of the women folks," grinning as he looked at Cord.

Cord glanced to the dusty road, seeing the easily identifiable shoes of the Andalusian, not just from the cleats of the shoes, but the length of the stride and the often double stepped tracks. It was the way of the Andalusian, especially any that were trained by the Mexican vaqueros who prided themselves in what they called the *Charreria* for the magnificent animals. It was a special dance step taught the horses and when the vaqueros gathered for a *Charreria*, there was always music.

The stagecoach road from Idaho Springs had a considerable grade and the big stallion leaned into the climb, the mule tugging on his lead, and Blue leading the way. After about a half mile, the road bent to the northwest and continued its climb but it was easier going. With an occasional glance to the tracks in the dust, Cord was confident the man was bound for Black Hawk. The sudden rattle of trace chains and the thunder of hooves from behind him, made Cord turn in his saddle and see a stage coming up the grade after him. He nudged Kwitcher to the uphill shoulder of the road, stopping to let the stage pass.

The driver and messenger nodded and waved as they passed, the driver focusing on the work of handling the six-up of mules, and Cord saw a stage load with extra passengers seated atop while every window showed passengers within. He waited until the dust settled, then nudged Kwitcher back to the road. While he usually preferred trails in the trees, the steep hillsides and thick timber of the canyon made any game trails more challenging than he wanted, especially since he wanted to follow Chapo and the Andalusian, that horse was the bait and Cord was determined to find Malcolm and make him pay the consequences of his outlaw ways.

But the road bent back on itself and Cord could hear the rattling and rumbling of the stage well above him but screened by the heavy timber. After another switchback, the road began to climb from the bottom of Virginia Canyon to cross the face of the north slopes of the mountains, winding around the protruding shoulders, but ever climbing higher. The road bent through Buttermilk Gulch, and over the mountain shoulders, dipping in and out of the gulches and draws. Cord began to appreciate the beauty of the mountains, and even with a bit of dust in the air from the coach, he breathed deeply of the pungent smells of pine and quakies. The road cut into the south facing hills, often showing the opposing north facing hills to be more thickly timbered and appearing almost black, with south facing shoulders showing more quakies that fluttered in the morning air, showing off their pale green leaves and white bark.

The road made another switchback, cutting back on itself to cross the higher slopes of the mountains. The hillsides were scarred by several prospect holes, and after another switchback, ever climbing higher, the tailings of a good sized lode mine stood above the road, sometimes draining rainwater onto the road. Cord was still watching for the tracks of his quarry when he heard gunshots and thundering hooves and more. He frowned, moved to the point of a shoulder and craned to look at the road beyond. All he saw was dust rising from beyond the trees and no more shooting.

With a frown, he dug heels to Kwitcher and kicked the stallion up to a canter, the reluctant mule stretching out to keep pace. After rounding a couple more shoulders and dips in the road, he saw dust still rising from the drop off of a sharp curve. He quickly reined up, stepped down and went to the edge of the road, and saw what he did not want to see, the scattered and broken remains of the stage. He looked around, led the grulla and mule to the inside shoulder of the road and into the trees, giving them a bit of shade and a little grass. He took the riata from the loop on the pommel, shook his head as he turned back to the road.

Cord paused at the edge of the road, looking below over the sheer precipice of rocky cliff at the scattered debris and bodies. He shook his head, seeing what he could and deciding where to begin. Only concerned about the people, he climbed down, moving from rock escarpment to boulder to handholds on cliff ledges, he passed the debris that included valises and other bags split open, and contents, papers, clothing and more hanging from outcroppings and scattered about by both the crash and the mountain winds. He began working his way down the steep talus slope, carefully picking his way through the rocks, looking for anyone that could be helped. Two men were the first he came to, lying on the rocks, bloody and twisted in unnatural positions, lifeless eyes staring at the sun, clothing torn and dirty, and Cord thought they were peddlers or something of the sort with suits and linen shirts.

Another man, also dead and broken, head downhill, blood on the rocks and dirt, twisted and bent, face down in a split between two rocks, his head split and lying in a pool of blood. And so it went, until he heard a moan, turned to look at a nearby tree and saw color that was not natural. He moved closer, saw a pale blue splotch of material and heard another moan. As he neared, he guessed this was a woman and when he came close, saw she was face down. He grabbed her shoulder to roll her over, and saw a small child, maybe four or five, dirty face made so by dirt and tears. The little girl opened her frightened eyes and held out her arms to Cord, asking to be lifted up into his arms. Cord grabbed the little girl, lifted her from under her mother's bloody body, and turned her away, resting her head on his shoulder, and softly patting her back, speaking in low tones to soothe her.

Cord looked around, saw other bodies, but no other sign of life, and decided to climb back up and do something, but he did not know what, with the little girl. Once atop, he went to his animals and sat down by the big ponderosa that offered both shade and some soft grass. He cleaned up the little girl with water from his water bag and his neckerchief, dug out some jerky for her to chew on and was pleased when Blue lay down beside her and the dog and girl immediately became best friends. He chuckled, watching as the girl lay back, resting her head on Blue's chest as he stretched out, lying on his side behind her. She was quickly asleep, content with the dog. Cord sighed heavily, stood and walked away to return to the wreckage to look for any other survivors.

It was mid-afternoon when Cord finished his search of the wreckage. There were no other survivors and he left the wreckage and debris where it lay. He found three mules with broken legs or worse injuries and had to put them out of their misery with a shot to the head. All the others he found, were already dead. He counted nine bodies, only one woman, the girl's mother. He tried to cover the bodies with blankets, coats, or anything else he could find, but had neither the time nor the strength to bury them or bring the bodies up top. When he returned to find the little girl still sleeping with Blue, he smiled, led the horses back to the road, and lifted her to the saddle. He seated her in front of him and started on to Black Hawk. As he passed the sharp bend in the road, he saw the remains of a broken wagon wheel, a big one that had obviously come from the wagon Cord found below. As he looked at the sign, he guessed the wagon had stopped on the curve, surprised the coach, been warned by the gunshots, but were unable to stop or turn aside and went over the edge. *Maybe that's what happened, but it could have been anything and those that know aren't talking.* He had forgotten about those he followed and wondered if they had passed before or after the wreck. He nudged Kwitcher to a quick step and headed for Central City where he would report on the stage and let them take care of retrieving the bodies, but now he had a little girl to be concerned with, and he had no idea where to start.

11

CENTRAL CITY

As he neared the crest of the saddle, the hills were pockmarked with prospect holes that told of big dreams and shattered hopes, leaving behind piles of rubble dug from the mountainside. The road bent through the black timber, Kwitcher taking his time but walking with head high and ears pricked as he watched Blue scouting the trail before them. The air turned cool, coming up the mountain from the north and whispering through the trees. Cord opened his duster and wrapped it around the child who snuggled back against him, seeking warmth as well as comfort and protection. She had not said a word since he carried her from the bottom of the cliff face and lay her on the grass with Blue, but she seemed to be alert and attentive.

As Cord watched the trail, she squirmed around, asking, "Are you my daddy?"

Cord was startled by the question and stammered, "Uh, no, my name's Cord, what's yours?"

"I'm Marybel, Marybel Potter an' I'm fo' years old!" she declared, twisting around and bending back to look at Cord.

"Marybel, huh, I had a sister by that name. You lookin' for your daddy? Expect to find him in Central City or Black Hawk?"

"Dunno. Momma said he was a gold miner and we was gonna find him."

"What's his name?"

"Daddy," declared Marybel, pursing her lips and nodding her head as if she made a royal pronouncement that would bear no doubting.

Cord let a slow smile split his face as he glanced down to the golden curls that covered her head and framed her face. Rosy cheeks with freckles and dimples added to the cuteness and her confident manner told of a strong personality. Even though her name was the same as Cord's sister, there was no resemblance between the two, at least not that Cord could remember. His sister had dark, bobbed hair much like his, no dimples but ample freckles, and a quiet manner that kept her hidden behind her mother's skirts. Cord sighed heavily with the memory and looked through the break of the trees to the hills below.

As the trees opened up to show the hills, a big basin lay before him, the hills all about had been denuded leaving rocks and stumps to decorate the otherwise bald hillsides. The trees had been cut to build houses, businesses, shoring for mines, and fire-wood, leaving behind scarred landscapes dotted by random log cabins, prospect holes and other debris. Men that were searching for gold saw no need of cleaning up after their leavings, preferring to spend the time and energy in their search for riches.

Cord rode at the edge of the stage road, often looking in the dust for the tracks of the Mex and the big black Andalusian horse, and he was relieved to see the unmistakable tracks of the big black, but the wind had started to cover the tracks, he was still hopeful of finding enough sign to tell whether he went to Nevadaville, Central City, or Black Hawk. With many trails and roads going every which way, signs were erected to point the way to the different lodes or mines and settlements. When the road crossed the basin and climbed the face of the low shoulder of the far mountain, a sign pointing up a long draw to the west told of Nevadaville. Other signs told the locations of lodes like Bates Lode, Gunnell Mine, Burroughs Lode, Bobtail Lode and others.

As he rounded another shoulder of the butte, the road opened up and showed the makings of a town that Cord guessed to be Central City. Log cabins dotted the scarred hillsides, others lined the road and as the town rose up the road was lined with false fronted business buildings on both sides, lettered windows, signs and more proclaiming the names and types of business. Cord spotted a two-story building with a covered porch that held a balcony above and a sign saying *St. Charles Hotel,* and across the road was the *Big Barn Livery and Blacksmith,* but the closer building was more what Cord was looking for, *Roworth Brothers Store, Mercantile, Groceries and Mining Supplies.* He reined up in front of the store, swung a leg over the cantle and stepped down, reached up to lift Marybel down and after tethering the animals and telling Blue, "Stay here with Kwitcher and the mule," stepped up on the boardwalk and pushed into the store.

Cord heard a woman's voice, "Welcome friend, how may we help you?"

Cord walked to the counter where the aproned woman stood, hands on hips, smiling and looking at Cord and down to Marybel, "Well, what have we here? You're a pretty little thing, what's your name?"

"I'm Marybel, an' I'm fo' years old!" declared the little blonde, smiling.

"Four years old! My, my, my, and is this your daddy?" she asked, motioning to Cord.

"No," she stated, glancing up at Cord. "He took me from my momma."

The woman stepped back, frowning, "You did what?" she growled, hands back on her hips as she leaned back as if about to launch a tirade against the man before her.

Cord held up his hands, palms out, to defend

himself, "Now, hold on, it's not like that! Let me explain!" he declared.

"Well, you better!" she pronounced.

"The stagecoach coming from Idaho Springs collided with a freight wagon and they both went off the cliff. I'm afraid Marybel is the only survivor. I came to tell somebody about it so some folks can go retrieve or bury the bodies."

The woman stepped back, hand to her mouth as her eyes flared wide, "Oh my goodness! That's, that's terrible!"

"Yes'm, it certainly was, and Marybel said she was looking for her daddy, fella name of Potter, she says his first name is 'Daddy' "

The woman turned and called out, "Rufus! Rufus, come here this instant!"

An aproned man came from the back room, carrying a box of something as he looked around at the woman, "What is it, Martha?"

"Put that down! I'm going to take this dear child to our home while this man goes over to see Sheriff Glennan." She began untying her apron and reached out to Marybel, "C'mon honey, let's go get you something to eat and get you some fresh clothes." She looked at Cord, "The sheriff's office is across the street, two doors down from the hotel. You go on now, us womenfolk will take care of each other!"

Cord looked at Marybel, "Is that all right, Marybel? For you to go with Martha here?"

"Ummhmm. But you'll come back, won't you?"

"Sure I will, right after I see the sheriff."

Marybel nodded, accepted the offered hand from Martha and turned away as Cord started to the door.

As he stepped out of the store, Cord shook his head and said, "No wonder I ain't married, a woman like that and I'd never have any peace!" He walked across the road, took to the boardwalk in front of the hotel and walked past the hotel, the lawyer's office, saw the sign that read, *Sheriff Richard Glennan,* and pushed into the office. The man behind the desk was a long lanky type, with a hatchet face and a hook nose, but his expression was all business as he looked up at Cord. "What's the problem?"

"What makes you think there's a problem?"

"Strangers don't come into the sheriff's office less'n there's a problem. What's yours?"

"Not mine, exactly. But I came across the stage from Idaho Springs back up the trail a ways. It went off the road on a curve above a sheer drop-off. It looked like it had a full load when it passed me earlier, but I went down, checked it out, only one lived. A little girl that Mrs. Roworth took to her home," he nodded across the street toward the store.

The sheriff frowned, "What caused it?"

"Dunno for sure, didn't see it, but from the tracks it looks like a freight wagon had a wheel break 'bout the time they was to pass or sumpin'. Both of 'em went o'er the edge. Made quite a mess. Thought maybe you'd like to get some men together, go get the bodies or bury 'em or sumpin'."

"Was the stage carryin' anything important?"

"Other than people? Dunno, after I found the little girl, didn't have time to do no lookin' for anything but to see if there were any others still alive, but there weren't."

"How many?"

"Oh, a dozen or less."

The sheriff frowned, shaking his head, looked back at Cord, "What's your name and what're you here for?"

"Name's Cordell Beckett. I'm here lookin' for somebody."

"What'chu want with him?"

"That's my business, Sheriff. But if you've seen a man, big fella, fancy dresser, likes black, wears a lotta silver, that might be the one."

"Yeah, I saw a fella like that get off the stage the other day. Went to the hotel there," nodding up the street to the St. Charles.

"Thanks, Sheriff. What about the little girl?"

"What about her? Din't you say Mrs. Roworth had her?"

"That's right, but I kinda feel responsible for her, we kinda became friends on the way down. So, I'm concerned about her. You know any man by the name of Potter?"

The sheriff frowned, thinking, "Potter, sounds familiar, but..." he shrugged, "Dunno. I'll hafta ask around." He rose from behind his desk, grabbed his hat off the hook by the door and followed Cord out.

"Well, we probably won't head out till in the mornin', since you said there were no survivors, so, I'll get some men together, you wanna come with us, show us where it happened?"

"You won't have any trouble finding it - sharp curve, steep drop off, you'll find it all right. It'll be dark soon, and my horse is tired, too tired to make that jaunt again, and I'd like to get a bath and some food also. I might check with you in the morning, though."

The sheriff nodded, understanding and started across the street as Cord turned away bound for the Big Barn livery, then the store to check on Marybel and on to the hotel.

12

SEARCH

"There he is!" declared the tiny voice of the little girl as she came running toward Cord. He had just stepped into the store and was surprised to see her in a new frilly dress, hair combed and pinned back, her curls bouncing as she ran with a wide smile and freckles and dimples showing. Her arms spread wide, she jumped into Cord's arms and giggled. "You like my new dress?"

Cord chuckled, "It is mighty pretty, but not as pretty as you!" Cord declared, holding her on his hip, and laughing. He looked to see a stern-faced Martha Roworth marching toward him and prepared himself for some sort of remonstration.

"You put her down, right now! I'll not have some worthless saddle tramp getting her all worked up!"

"Now hold on a minute, me'n Marybel are the best of friends!" declared Cord, turning away from Martha, and putting Marybel out of reach.

"My Rufus and I are going to find her *real* father and if he can't be found, well then, we will take her as our own!" She made her declaration with her hand on her hips, her eyes full of fire, and a stomp of her foot to emphasize her profound declaration.

Cord looked from the woman to Marybel and asked, "Is that what you want Marybel?"

The tyke grew very serious as she fiddled with Cord's collar, and said in her tiny voice, "She's been nice to me, but I want my daddy."

"Well, we all are going to do our best to find your daddy, but I'll be movin' around a bit and won't have a good place for you to stay and sleep, but Mrs. Roworth here, she wants you to stay with her," Cord looked at the woman and with a stern expression as he glared at her but spoke to Marybel, "and she promises to take real good care of you. She has a nice place for you to sleep, and she's a good cook and will have good food for you."

He was interrupted by the child, "Will I get cupcakes?"

Cord chuckled, looked to a nodding and smiling Martha, and answered, "Yes, she'll even let you help her make the cupcakes. Now doesn't that sound fine?"

"Will you come see me?" she asked, her head tilted down and her eyes lowered.

"Yes! I'll come see you just as often as I can, but first, we'll be trying to find your daddy."

"All right," she said as she wiggled to be free.

Cord put her down and she toddled over to Martha who took her hand and turned away from Cord to take Marybel back to their home. Cord watched them go, turned away and walked out onto the boardwalk for a quick look around.

He went back to the hotel, anticipating a good supper and a night's rest in a bed. He smiled at the thought, stepped into the hotel and walked through the lobby to go to the dining room. He stood in the doorway, looking at the diners at the tables, saw an empty table on the far side and walked to it. He slipped off his duster, hung it on the empty chair, doffed his hat and sat it on the same chair as he seated himself with his back to the wall. He had no sooner taken a seat, than a pretty redhead with a frilly apron came with a coffee pot and a cup and with a smile, asked, "Coffee?"

"Sure," answered Cord, "What's the special?"

"Well, we have several, there's turkey with cranberry sauce, filet of beef braised with mushrooms, and scrambled hog's brains with butter. Oh, and there's broiled quail with toast."

Cord frowned, "Uh, I'll have the beef, thank you."

"That will be right out, sir," she answered.

As she started to turn away, Cord stopped her with a raised hand and asked, "Uh, miss. I'm lookin' for a man, might have been in today or yesterday. He's older'n me, big fella, fancy dresser, likes black and silver, fancies himself quite the ladies' man."

She scowled, "Yes! He was in earlier and he was

rude and horrible!" she spoke through clinched teeth. She dipped her head a little and looked at Cord from under her brows, "Is he a friend of yours?"

Even if he was, with that response Cord would have said no, but he said, "No, why?"

"He tried to grab me! I have a beau and told him so, but he didn't care. I had to slap his hand and run away! I never..." she pursed her lips and slowly shook her head. Cord would not have been surprised to see steam come from her ears. She added, "He is staying at the hotel and I hope I do not have to see him again! When he left, he went up the street where the taverns are and I hope he does not come back!"

"You have a beau, good for you."

She breathed easier, stood a little taller and lifted her head, "Yes, I do. And we'll be married just as soon as we can."

"Let me guess. He's a prospector, found some color, expects to strike it rich any day now?" said Cord, a slight smile tugging at his mouth.

She lifted her head again, "No, he's not. He works at the new smelter and once it is up and running, which will be any day now, he'll make good money and we can get married."

"Well, congratulations, I'm happy for you."

"Thank you, sir," she smiled and turned back to the kitchen.

After she cheerfully served his meal, Cord ate in silence, thoughtful about what he had learned about Jerry Malcolm. He was in town, staying at the same hotel, but now was in one of the taverns probably setting himself up to try his outlaw ways again, maybe recruit some men and lay his plans to take over claims and rob the miners. Cord chuckled to himself, thinking about what he would do, knowing it would not be an easy thing, but he thought he might use the black horse to accomplish his purpose, keep any confrontation away from the crowds.

Central City and Black Hawk had experienced sudden and rapid growth in the years before the war, but with much of the placer gold taken, that growth stalled during the war. Now with new means and methods of lode mining and with the stamping mills showing some success at separating the gold from quartz and other minerals, it looked like the towns would again enjoy growth and prosperity. Apparently, that was what had appealed to Malcolm, anywhere there was gold to be had and miners to be fleeced, he was determined to do the fleecing. But Cord was also concerned about the other men that had ridden with the Red Legs; Newt Morrison, Jerry Malcolm, Bill Coogan, and Buck Smithers. Where were they?

When Cord stepped out of the hotel onto the boardwalk, he shrugged into his duster, turned the collar up, pulled the brim of his hat down, and faded into the shadows of the dusk. Shafts of light showed from windows, angling to the boardwalks, but the shadows before the closed businesses and empty buildings wrapped Cord in the darkness as he walked up the bending main road that slowly climbed the low hill where the raucous crowds of the taverns shouted and danced to the tinpanny pianos and the titillating screams of the women. Cord stopped beside the window of the first tavern, weather worn boards showing grey, fly-specked windows masked the view, but Cord could see the crowd, most of the men were at the tables, watching as cards were dealt and chips were hoarded. But there was no big man in black.

He moved on to the Big Nugget, the biggest saloon and the loudest, but the windows were covered with curtains and Cord pushed through the swinging doors, paused to let his eyes get accustomed to the light, then walked to the long bar, finding a place at the end. With a nod to the barkeep, he ordered a mug of beer and stood with elbows on the bar and face turned down, but eyes roving all about.

At a table near the window, Cord spotted Malcolm. He was sitting with his back to the corner, but he was holding court. His hat was pushed back from his brow, the silver band showing in the light, his broad smile laughed as he pushed a stack of chips into the pot while he looked around at the others. There were five other men at the table, none were laughing, most were grim and stoic, but four of the five also added chips while one man folded his cards and leaned back, glancing to Malcolm.

The dealer answered the call of each man,

dealing the requested cards and accepting the
throwaways, then dealt his own, and lifting them
before his face, he shuffled through the cards, then
slowly fanned the cards to see what he had. He
looked at Malcolm who was grinning and laughing
as he reached for more chips. Although Cord was not
a gambler, he had learned many of the tricks of the
card sharps about hidden cards, and more. He
watched Malcolm as he held his cards before him,
fanning and shuffling them as he watched the
others. He would often hold his cards in one hand,
but put his hands together, elbows on the table,
allowing his fingers to be within reach of his shirt
cuffs that sported silver cuff links that were eye
catchers and a distraction. Cord chuckled, knowing
the trick, but he did not see Malcolm make a move,
yet he also knew that a good cheat was slick and not
easily followed. But the response of the others when
the hand was called and Malcolm lay down his cards,
fanned out, to show his winning hand of a full house,
aces over queens, the reaction of the others was
anger and disgust, prompting two of the men to rise
and walk away in a rage, shaking their heads and
mumbling to themselves. But Malcolm slipped his
silver-mounted pearl-handled pistol from the holster
and lay it on the table before him, glanced around
the table and watched the two men walk away.

One of the men slammed his way out the doors,
and within moments, came back in the same way,
but with a rifle in his hands. He was glaring at the

table in the corner, and stomped his way toward it, shouting at Malcolm, "You're a sneakin' cheat!" his rifle held before him, but the blast of a pistol shattered the follies and the bullet took the man in his upper chest, splitting his breastbone and driving him back, stumbling over the feet of the men at the nearest table, and falling to his back, dead where he fell. The crowd had been silenced, and no one moved as they looked from the table where Malcolm, now standing and grinning as he held his pistol with its thin trail of smoke lifting from the muzzle, then to the man on the floor.

Cord shook his head, reached for his mug of beer and watched the crowd. Someone shouted, "Better go get the sheriff!"

The barkeep motioned to a man at the far end of the bar and the two went to the downed man, looked at the wound and the face of the man and looked up at the gathering crowd, "He's dead, sure 'nuff."

13

CONFRONTATION

THE SHERIFF PUSHED HIS WAY THROUGH THE CROWD, HIS tall lanky frame and hatchet face with the big nose that entered the room first, was recognized by all and Cord watched the crowd as they moved away, allowing the sheriff to enter. Cord noticed the instant respect most of the men showed the lean figure of a man, apparently he had established himself as a no nonsense sheriff and most gave him a wide berth. He wore canvas trousers, a linsey Woolsey shirt and brown leather vest with the badge pinned over the breast pocket, and a tall-crowned, brown felt hat, on his hip rode a holstered Remington Army revolver converted to metallic cartridges in .46 caliber. It took a man to handle the big Remington and Glennan seemed to be just the sort of man that could make good use of such a weapon.

He knelt down by the body, looked at the hole in the chest and the rifle laying to the side, he looked at those standing around and asked, "Did he have that in his hands when he was shot?"

"Yeah, yeah, he did, Sheriff! He had been in the card game yonder," nodding to the table where Malcolm still stood, "left an' came back in with his rifle. Called that man yonder a sneakin' cheat, and 'fore he could lift the rifle, that man in black there, shot him plumb center!"

The others standing nearby mumbled their agreement, nodding and pointing toward Malcolm. Cord had turned to face the confrontation, his elbow on the bar and the mug of beer in his hand as he watched. The sheriff rose, and Cord watched Malcolm holster his pistol and sit down, reach for his cards as if he was going to continue playing, but the sheriff stepped closer, standing between Malcolm and Cord. "What'chu got to say 'bout it?" growled the sheriff, his arms folded across his chest.

"Well, just like the man said. That'n," nodding to the dead man, "came stormin' in, waving his rifle, called me a cheat and I beat him to the shootin'. Had to, otherwise that'd be me layin' on the floor in my own blood."

The others at the table were looking from one to the other and Cord saw fear in their eyes as Malcolm looked at each one, his eyes showing danger as his nostrils flared and one eyebrow cocked, daring each one to contradict what he said. But no one countered what Malcolm said, although most answered with meek voices, none looking at Malcolm, and glancing from the sheriff to the body.

The sheriff turned away from the table, looked around the room, "Anybody else got anything different to say?" he called out loud enough to be heard by all.

No one answered and the sheriff started to leave when he heard a voice say, "You might wanna check the shooter's trail. You'll find a long line of dead bodies from Missouri to Colorado Territory and over at Oro City, California Gulch, and more."

Few, other than the sheriff, heard what had been said by Cord and the sheriff stepped closer to Cord, "And why should I do that? Check his trail, I mean. All that's outta my jurisdiction."

"Ummhmm, but might help you understand whatever's gonna be happenin' around here 'fore too long," added Cord, lifting his mug to take a quaff of beer.

The sheriff grunted, turned away and stomped out the door with a brief glance over his shoulder at Cord as he disappeared in the darkness.

As the crowd settled down, several calling for refills on their drinks, Malcolm scowled and raised his voice to be heard across the tavern, "You there! You that was talkin' to the sheriff, what were you sayin' to him?" It was an angry and threatening tone used by Malcolm, who was used to other men paying attention to him, and it riled him that the man in the duster at the bar paid him no mind.

Cord glanced toward Malcolm, but his hat brim was pulled low and his duster collar up and all that could be seen was the dark shadow of a whiskered face. Cord answered in a normal tone, "I was talkin' to the sheriff, not you!" and he turned his back to Malcolm to set the mug down and lean both elbows on the bar. He heard the ruckus from the table as Malcolm rose, kicking his chair back, and pushing and stomping his way toward Cord. As most bars have mirrors behind the racks of bottles, Cord watched as Malcolm approached, his hand on the butt of his pistol as he growled, "Don't turn your back on me!"

The others in the tavern had stopped talking and watched what was happening, but none moved to interfere. Cord sensed, rather than saw, as Malcolm neared and reached to grab Cord by the shoulder. Cord was ready, and as the hand touched him, he slapped his hand on Malcolm's, spun around and grasped Malcolm's hand in both of his, lifting it high and with Malcolm's arm stretched at length, Cord twisted his arm, driving Malcolm's face to the bar with his arm behind him, raised to its full length, his hand twisted around and fingers spread. The pain was instant and severe, totally controlling Malcolm who winced as Cord held the arm and hand stiff and high.

Cord saw Malcolm trying to grab his pistol with his free hand and Cord said, "Don't do it! I'll break your arm!" But Malcolm thought himself invincible and had always out-gunned any opponent or at least bluffed his way through. But when he grabbed the pistol and started to lift it from the holster, Cord brought Malcolm's arm straight down and the crack of the breaking arm was heard throughout the big room. Others winced at the sound and the pain as Malcolm screamed and dropped to his knees, knocking over the brass spittoon that splashed over his legs and jacket. But his only thought was to retaliate and he dragged the Remington from the holster and tried to twist around to bring it to bear, but Cord brought up his knee under Malcolm's chin, knocking him backward into the puddle of spittle and spewed tobacco. He was unconscious, laying limp as blood dripped from his mouth.

Cord turned away, "Somebody might wanna get a doctor or sumpin'. An' if you think he was dangerous, you might wanna be gone when he comes to." Cord flipped a coin to the bar top to pay for his beer, turned and pushed through the crowd to return to his hotel room. He was anxious to get that night's rest in a good bed. But the sheriff had not gone back to his office, instead he waited outside on the boardwalk on the bench by the window. As Cord neared, he looked up and asked, "Was that you makin' all that noise?"

"Had a little misunderstanding with a fella."

"He the one you were lookin' for?"

Cord nodded, leaned against the post that held

the overhang of the saloon and hung its shadow over the bench where the sheriff sat. "He's the one."

"Why were you lookin' for him?"

"Like I said, he left a trail behind of dead bodies and more."

"Any of 'em personal?"

"My family in Missouri, most of those 'tween here an' there were folks that had money that he wanted, or here in the gold fields, both gold dust and claims that he thought he should have."

"He do all that by himself?"

"Nope, but most o' them have already paid their due."

"And you're the collector?"

"You might say that," answered Cord, looking at the dark sky with the sliver of silvery moon hanging in the west. There were few stars that showed themselves, their lanterns apparently masked by heavy cloud cover that boded storms.

"What gives you the right?" asked the sheriff.

Cord turned back to look at the man and slipped his marshal badge from his vest pocket, held it in the palm of his hand and let the light from the window of the tavern reflect on it as he showed it to the sheriff. Glennan frowned, looked up at Cord, "Suits me."

The sheriff stood, looked up and down the street, "You din't kill him, didju?"

"No, just bent his arm a little."

The sheriff nodded, "Let me walk you to your hotel, just in case you got any other ideas 'bout folks.

I like a peaceable town." He glanced to Cord, "I take it since you don't wear that badge on your chest, that you're sorta incognito?"

"Ummhmm," answered Cord with a slight smile splitting his face.

"I like a peaceable town," responded the sheriff.

"Me too."

"That was my way of sayin' I'd just as soon see you leave."

"I will sheriff, just as soon as I find out where the others are, he might have been plannin' to meet up with 'em here in Central City, but I'm thinkin' more like Black Hawk."

The sheriff huffed, mumbled, "Hope it's Black Hawk."

14

PROMONTORY

Cord was at the Big Barn Livery before first light. He regretted his confrontation with Malcolm the night before but it could not be helped. He still believed Malcolm was the key to finding the other Jayhawkers that had killed his family. Still struggling with his quest for vengeance or justice, he did not believe he accomplished either with his encounter with Malcolm. Cord still thought the black horse of Malcolm's would be the answer, believing the man would not leave the horse behind and would probably want to leave Central City after his embarrassing encounter with Cord last night.

He went to the stalls for his grulla and the mule, began saddling and rigging the animals. The black was still in the livery and the sleepy liveryman had returned to his room, grumbling all the way. When Cord rode from the livery, he saw little life on the streets of Central City, with a glance to the store where Marybel stayed with Martha, he tipped his hat as he passed, remembering the smiling little blonde who had been reclaimed by her father, but would still be staying with Martha until her father could fix them a cabin to live in near his claim.

The road to Black Hawk was lined with remnants of placer claims, cabins, and more. With the rising sun climbing into the notch of the mountains, the warmth on his face, Cord noticed the many pock marks of prospect holes on the hillsides that rose from the creek bed. Off his right shoulder was the bigger ore dump from one of the more successful mines, while most were small dumps made by a single man searching for his lode. The creek bed had been dug, washed, sifted through and re-routed by the placer miners over the past five or six years since the first discovery in '59. Stumps, weathered log cabins, and other debris littered the hillsides scattered among the prospect holes and dumps. He was alone on the road until he heard the clatter of hooves and the rattle of trace chains behind him. He moved to the side to let the rumbling ore wagon pass, knowing it was bound for the new smelter in Black Hawk. He had learned about the area and believed this was what the Jayhawker bunch was looking for, the surge in mining with the new stamping mills and smelter promised to bring new prosperity to the area. And with prosperity came opportunity for outlaws to enrich themselves at the expense of the hard working miners. And now that Malcolm was a little incapacitated, he would be more apt to recruit new followers and begin their practice of outlawry.

He was east of Central City and the hillside on the south of the creek showed aspen and pine that had been untouched by the boomtown ways. He nudged Kwitcher to the trees, hoping to find an area that afforded him a view of the road below, yet cover and graze for the animals. When he took an old game trail that paralleled the road, he pushed into the edge of a cluster of mature aspen with tall trees, wide branches, and more space beneath that offered patches of grass and when he heard the chuckle of cascading water, he grinned, reined up and stepped down. He spotted a shoulder of rock that jutted above some of the trees that would make a good promontory to view the travelers on the road, and with graze and water, he believed he found his temporary camp, at least for a while.

On the upper edge of his chosen site, ponderosa and lodgepole pine were thick and black, and would make a better spot for his bedroll. A glance to the sky told him there would probably be rainfall before the day was full, and he began cutting some branches to weave a lean-to for shelter, but he would also use his canvas for cover. After his puttering around, he had his lean-to underneath a big ponderosa for extra protection, a good stack of firewood for his campfire and necessary coffee, and his gear stashed and handy. He heard another ore wagon passing on the road below and with Spencer and binoculars in hand, he went to his promontory and began his vigil.

The sheriff had told him that Malcolm had been taken to the sawbones and had been patched up and from what was reported, Malcolm was fuming and vowing revenge with every breath. "So, I'm glad to hear you're leavin'. I got 'nuff trouble without you an' Malcolm bein' a bother!" declared the sheriff as Cord left the hotel as the sheriff was coming into the dining room for his breakfast. Cord chuckled at the thought, and had made the sheriff keep the knowledge of Cord being a marshal under his hat, and the sheriff readily agreed.

Cord thought that Malcolm might give himself a day or two before leaving Central City because of his broken arm and more, but a man that is driven by anger and revenge seldom indulges in rest and patience. Cord himself knew those same emotions intimately, but he had been arguing and fussing with himself for some time now, and his struggle had been brought on by the argument offered by Reverend John Dyer, the snowshoe itinerant that had accompanied him on his jaunt to Denver City for the storekeeper in Oro City when he also gained his appointment as a federal marshal. The Reverend Dyer prompted Cord to examine the scripture about vengeance and revenge and judgment, and so far, it had been a disconcerting study.

As he sat on his promontory, he slipped the weathered Bible from his coat pocket and opened it to some of the earmarked pages. He started with a favorite of the Reverend, Psalm 111:10 *The fear of the Lord is the beginning of wisdom: a good understanding have all they that do his commandments: his praise endureth forever.* Cord remembered the preacher saying, "Fear - that's respect, honor, belief, and more. So much so that it feels much like what we know of as fear - you know, when your gut turns over and the prickles move up your spine, your breath comes in short gasps, like when you see an avalanche coming down the mountain, or a man holds a gun on you. Because when we have that feeling when we're close to God, it tells us we should be doing what He would want us to do."

When Cord allowed himself to reflect on his life and purpose, he struggled with his quest, *"Am I looking for revenge - to see them suffer and bleed and die like they did to my family? Or is Justice what I'm wanting - to see them held accountable for their murdering and robbing ways?"* He tried to think it was the latter, but the anger that often welled up within when he thought of what had happened, he struggled with the idea of just seeing justice, he wanted to strike out and make them feel what he felt.

He looked down at the Bible as the breeze from the mountains fanned the pages, he was not one that just let the Bible fall open, or let the pages turn, and think that was what was needed, but he preferred to search it out and let the Spirit of God guide his study. He lifted the Bible before him, turned to the earmarked pages and looked to John 5:30 *"I can of mine own self do nothing: as I hear, I judge: and my judgment is just, because I seek not own will, but the will of the Father which hath sent me."* And then to Romans 1:32 *"Who knowing the judgment of God, that they which commit such things are worthy of death, not only do the same, but have pleasure in them that do them."* He chuckled to himself, *I like that'n better.*

By mid-day and after watching all the movement on the road below, Cord retreated from his overlook and with his fire under the overhanging branches, he brewed up some coffee and cooked some beans and bacon for his lunch. From his cookfire, he could see through the quakies enough to spot any movement on the road, concerned only by single riders or two or three traveling together. But by the end of the day when dusk lowered its curtain, Malcolm had not taken the road to Black Hawk and Cord was ready to turn into his blankets. There had been a light drizzle during the afternoon, but the black clouds and distant thunder warned of more and Cord made a last check of his lean-to and turned in for the night.

The storm charged up the valley of the North fork of Clear Creek, the downpour washing the hillsides and cutting rivulets across the hillsides already scarred by the work of prospectors and soon North Clear Creek was running high with muddy runoff water crowding over the embankments and tearing at the road and skirts of the hills. Muddy water cascaded down the hillsides and the crashing and roaring of the floodwaters had chased birds and animals to their dens and nests and the creek carried the muddy water with tons of debris, brush, logs, trees, sluice boxes, and more as it crashed down the valley.

Cord's handiwork on his lean-to held, with the laced branches, the canvas cover, and the strong frame, as well as with the protecting overhanging branches of the big ponderosa, he was secure. But sleep was not possible with the echoing roar of the thunder, the crashing clap of lightning, and the ever-increasing roar of floodwaters; there was no peace nor sleep to be had.

15

BLACK HAWK

When the grey light of early morning made a silhouette of the horizon, the bowl of the moon, now waxing toward full, hung in the cloudy sky. The grey bottomed clouds promised additional storms, and the distant rumble bode thunder and lightning. Cord rolled from his blankets and crawled from under the lean-to, looking through the quakies to the muddy excuse for a road below. No life showed anywhere, the only sounds being the gurgle and chuckle of the remaining floodwaters as they tumbled down the mountainside, searching for the escape in the creek below.

Cord stood, stretching, breathing deep of the fresh cool air. As the morning breeze began to whisper through the quakies, droplets of water tumbled from the quivering leaves to add their moisture to the muddy soil. Cord pulled the Bible from under the lean-to, grabbed his Spencer, and climbed the rocks to his promontory to watch the road below.

As the sun slowly climbed over his right shoulder to lay its golden lances down the length of the valley, Cord began reading in Romans 12. He did as do many, read without paying close attention, too distracted by his surroundings, until he came to verse *17 "Recompense to no man evil for evil,"* he paused, re-read the passage and skipped ahead, *"live peaceably with all men, Dearly beloved, avenge not yourselves, but rather give place unto wrath, for it is written, Vengeance is mine, I will repay, saith the Lord."* He stopped, looked at the verses again, and lifted his face to Heaven, "God, what are you tryin' to tell me?" he did not really want to get an answer. It had been so much easier just picking his own way and justification for his vengeance quest. He struggled with the thought, arguing with himself about justice and vengeance. But he felt the weight of the badge in his pocket, considering his search from a different point of view, knowing he had taken an oath to uphold the law and that law required him to bring the suspected outlaws to face justice. He breathed deep, looking around, saw a freight wagon with a four-up harness of mules struggling in the muddy road below.

He dropped his eyes and began his usual time of prayer, asking the oft-asked question for God to give him the guidance in his search for those that had killed his family and more. It was the crack of the bullwhip that brought his attention back to those below and he saw a lone rider on a big black horse, moving past an ore wagon. He immediately recognized Jerry Malcolm, riding east toward Black Hawk. This was what Cord was waiting for; hopefully Malcolm would lead him to the others that had been a part of the raid on his family's place. He climbed down from the escarpment, started to saddle his mount, but paused, thinking, and decided to have some breakfast before leaving, not wanting to reveal himself to Malcolm before time.

Black Hawk was more developed than Central City, due to the presence of the stamping mills and the newly constructed smelter by the Boston and Colorado Smelting Company, that was showing considerable success in separating the gold from the sulfides with their improved process, thanks to a Brown University professor, Nathaniel Hill. With two streets of business buildings, the new prosperity was showing itself with the continual construction of more buildings, and many of them two stories and built of brick and stone, giving the air of permanence and prosperity.

Cord chuckled as he rode into the town, knowing this was exactly what Malcolm and his cronies would be wanting. Not just successful businesses, but the wealth that drew more prospectors and in their minds, more targets for their taking. He rode to the sheriff's office, noticed the name on the door of C.M. Grimes and pushed into the small office that was backed by a row of jail cells, several occupied. A man looked up from the desk, "Yes?"

Cord stepped to the desk, extended his hand, "Are you Sheriff Grimes?"

The man shook his head, "Nope. I'm his deputy, Wilbur Stoddard. What'chu need?"

"Oh, just wanted to talk to the sheriff. When will he be back?"

"Don't rightly know. He rode out 'fore the storm hit, weren't plannin' on comin' back till next week, but..." he shrugged, turning his attention back to the newspaper, *Tri-Weekly Miner's Register.*

"Where'd you recommend stayin', you know, a hotel, maybe with a dining room?"

The man gave a lazy look up at Cord, pointed toward the lower end of the street, "The other side o' the street, around the corner, is the Gilpin. It's got both."

"And which saloon is the most popular with the miners?"

"Hennesey's."

Cord nodded, turned away and left the sheriff's office, grabbed the reins of Kwitcher and the lead of the mule and started walking down the edge of the street, looking around at the busy town. Buildings were under construction, the smell of sawdust in the air, people were moving about on the boardwalks, businesses appeared to be busy with doors standing wide open, and hitchrails held several hipshot horses. It appeared about every third or fourth business was a saloon and all appeared to be busy, even though it was still early in the day.

The Black Hawk Livery and Blacksmith was across the street from the hotel and Cord secured a stall for his animals, stripped their riggings and gave both a good brushing before forking them some hay from the loft. With the saddlebags over his shoulder and the Winchester in his hand, having secured his packs and other weapons in the livery storeroom, he walked across the street to get a room at the hotel. With his gear stashed, Cord left the hotel and went next door to the barber.

It was a busy place, with two chairs and barbers, both chairs with men under the big aprons and one with a face of shaving soap as the barber busied himself stropping the razor. Other men were seated on a long bench that stretched across the front of the shop, leaving the waiting customers with their backs to the big window. Cord seated himself, crossed his arms as he sat beside a husky bearded man that was obviously a miner with dusty clothes that had been strangers to any water or soap, both man and duds.

The barbers and their customers were talkers and Cord listened. Another man that sat on the long bench on the far side of the big miner was talking with one of the barbers, "So, we missed you in services Sunday, Paul."

The barber chuckled, "I know, Parson, but the wife wasn't feelin' too good, you know what with another'n on the way."

"What's that make now, Paul, four or five?"

"Now Parson, you know very well that's number six for us. We got more kids than most of the rest of the church combined!" he grumbled.

The first barber chuckled, talking to the man in his chair, "Apparently, Paul don't know what causes that!" a comment that elicited the laughter of the rest of the men. And when the laughter subsided, one of the other men added, "Maybe he needs to get some o' that religion the parson's always peddlin'!" which brought more laughter.

The parson gave a stern look to the talker and explained, "We don't *peddle* religion as you put it, John Dryden. Religion is man reaching up to God; Salvation is God reaching down to man! And that's exactly what *you* need, John."

"And what's the difference, Parson, I don't understand," replied John, leaning forward to see the Parson better.

"Well, John, religion is all the things people do to try to make themselves feel good, you know, hymn singing, fancy buildings, dressing a certain way, doing a litany of good deeds, all while trying to work their way to heaven. But the Bible says it's *'Not by works of righteousness which we have done, but according to his mercy he saved us, by the washing of regeneration and the renewing of the Holy Ghost.'* And that means He saves us when we go to Him, admit we're sinners, and ask for his mercy and the gift of eternal life, and He gives it just for the asking."

There was silence in the shop for just a few moments, until the one named John asked, "You mean I don't have to go to church to get to heaven?"

"John, you could go to every church in the country and that won't get you to heaven. It's that decision in your heart to trust God and Him alone, ask for forgiveness, and He will save you."

"So, if I do that, then I'll get my ticket to Heaven?"

"You could put it like that if you want, but if you do that, and truly mean it with all your heart, it *will* change your life. When you are saved by the grace of God, He gives you new life and it's called being born again. II Corinthians 5:17, says *'Therefore if any man be in Christ, he is a new creature, or a new creation. Old things are passed away, that means your old way of living, behold all things are become new'.*"

John looked around at the other men, the barbers, the two in the chairs and the others on the bench, "Any of you know what he's talkin' about, I mean, any of you ever done that, had that experience, you know?"

The other men sat still and silent, until the man with the soap on his face raised his hand and looked at John. Then the big miner beside Cord raised his, nodding his head in agreement, and Cord raised his just enough for the man to see.

He frowned, looking at the others, then back to the parson, "So, do I need to come to church to do that?"

"No, you can do it right here and right now, if you want. Or...you can wait until you're by yourself, or if you like, you can come with me afterward, and we'll talk some more."

"Yeah, that. I'll talk some more. Might have some more questions," mumbled John, dropping his eyes to the floor.

The barber by the second chair looked at his customer who was admiring the haircut in the mirror he held in his hand, and the barber asked, "So, now that the smelter is on line and workin', you think it's gonna do the job the other'n didn't?"

"It's already doin' the job. I think there's gonna be a long line of ore wagons at the smelter from now on, and there's gonna be more money flowin' in this town than there has been in the last several years!" declared the man, rising from the chair. He was a dapper-looking fella with a pinstripe suit, waistcoat, and spats over his shiny shoes. He reached into his pocket and brought out a coin, pressed it into the barber's hand and nodded, "And I thank you, Josiah. Until the next time?"

"Certainly Mr. Hill, thank you, sir."

Hill turned to the parson, "And Parson Averill, that is your church up on the hill there?"

Parson Averill nodded, "Yessir, it is, and you're welcome to join us."

"I just might do that," replied a nodding Nathaniel Hill as he exited the tonsorial parlor.

16

INVESTIGATION

HENNESEY'S TAVERN WAS THE POPULAR PLACE FOR MINERS, owners, and layabouts to congregate. Cord took his usual place at the end of the long bar that extended into the dark corner that in the daytime would be near a window, but now it was shadows and darkness. The dim light of the kerosene chandeliers and the lights at the back of the bar did little to push back the darkness, but Cord was satisfied with his place. Behind him and along the wall were tables that held talkers instead of players and he paid more attention to one that held three men when he entered, but now had gathered two more. They were hunkered over their drinks, and leaning close together. Because of the constant din of the gamblers and dancers, it was difficult to hear much, but he picked up on tidbits of conversation.

The man doing most of the talking was a big man with a lantern jaw, broad shoulders with a slight stoop, shifty dark eyes from under a broad brow and brown hair. Eyes that were constantly moving, looking about and a nervous twitch. But his deep growling voice commanded the attention of the others. At Cord's first glance, he saw the man dig a stub of a pencil from his pocket and wet it with his tongue, then with a scrap of paper before him, began drawing and explaining to the others. "Now, round 'chere, it's all gone to underground minin' an' there ain't no way we can do any good with that. Even if'n we was to take all the wagon loads of ore, it'd still need to go to the smelter 'fore they can get the gold out, and they ain't gonna give us the refined gold, seein' how they got five to ten guards for ever one of us.

"Now we allus done good when we took the lone miners, you know, them what's pannin' or sluicin' at the cricks. We can hit 'em with three or four men, take all they got, even get the papers on the claim an' take the claim, then sell it!" he cackled at the memory of doing that very thing.

"But if ever'thin's gone to underground, what're we gonna do?" pleaded the red head with the mottled complexion.

"Here's what I'm 'bout to show ya'. Now...," he leaned over the paper, looked around the table, and lowered his voice as he scratched on the paper. Cord heard bits and pieces...

"Russell gulch, an' Eureka Gulch gots..."

"An Lake gulch an' Chase Gulch has more..."

The talker leaned back, grinning at the others as they too relaxed and sat back in their chairs. The talker called out to the barkeep, "Bring us 'nother bottle!" and motioned him over.

Cord was nursing his mug of beer, elbows on the bar and shoulders hunkered, when the men at the table leaned in again and the speaker continued. "The way I got it figgered, after we make a run up the gulches, we can go to Nevadaville, or north to Rollinsville. An' if'n those don't suit, I heerd a fella talkin' bout Breckenridge and some new strikes down there, placer strikes. An' we can go there, it's back past Georgetown a ways, but..." he shrugged.

The second man asked, "But what's Malcolm gonna say?" the others around the table nodded and mumbled, leaned in for an answer.

"Don't know, don't care. He ain't here, so..." shrugged the big man, glaring at the others.

Cord stepped away from the bar and turned toward the door, wanting to get a better look at the men, believing some were part of the Jayhawkers. He pushed through the crowd, glanced at the table and knew two of the men, but did not get a look at the others. The big man that was holding court, he recognized as Newt Morrison, the self-appointed leader in the absence of Jerry Malcolm. And the redhead with the mutton-chop whiskers made him think of Red Clark, but Red had been killed. This man must be new but seemed to take the place of Red, not only in appearance but as the one that always stood in the shadow of Morrison. The others he did not get a good look at and what he saw was not familiar.

As Cord pushed his way through the crowd, he saw the swinging doors slap back and a familiar figure enter. His usual threatening glare was missing, but it was the same man, only this time he had his left arm in a tight sling and a scowl on his face as he looked around the smoke-filled room. Cord turned away, looking at the clerk with the sleeve garters spin the roulette wheel. He felt, rather than saw, Jerry Malcolm move past and push through the crowd toward the group at the table. He heard an outburst as those at the table spoke to the new arrival and chairs scraped the floor to make room for another.

Cord casually returned to the bar, taking an empty space away from the end, but a little closer to the table of the plotters. There was a door near the end of the bar that led to the outhouse out back and he started that direction, keeping his head turned toward the bar, using the mirror to see the men. They appeared to be welcoming Malcolm to their group, shaking hands and talking as Malcolm seated himself beside Newt Morrison, the two leaders sizing each other up. As Cord passed the table, he heard Malcolm explaining his injured arm as the result of his big black kicking him.

"But it'll be all right soon. Now..." he leaned forward and looked around the table. "What's been goin' on 'round here?"

Cord exited through the side door, walked down
the alley way to the main street to make his way back
to the hotel. Although he wanted to hear what was
said at the return of Malcolm, he did not want to
make himself familiar to the men. Even though
unknown, continued sighting and the accompanied
familiarity would raise suspicion, and he needed the
anonymity to accomplish his task. He returned to his
hotel room, turned in for the night, and lay with
hands behind his head, staring at the shadows on
the ceiling as he remembered and thought.

He was the first one in the dining room and as he
looked around, he chose the table near the window
and seated himself just as the waitress, a young
woman with long raven black hair and a disconcerting smile came to his table with a coffee pot, a
cup and a smile. Cord greeted her with a grin, "Good
morning miss. I'll have whatever the special is
today."

She poured his cup, glancing at him and said,
"It's cook's favorite, an omelet with eggs, ham,
bacon, cheese, hash browns, peppers and who knows
what all! There's also biscuits and gravy, and all the
coffee you can drink!"

Cord chuckled, nodded.

She looked around, lowered her voice and added,
"And if you want some apple pie, there's a little left
from last night!"

Cord grinned, "Well, if that omelet doesn't fill me up, I just might do that."

She smiled, nodded, and turned away to go to the kitchen.

He finished his breakfast, rose to leave as several others straggled into the dining room for their morning fare. He returned to his room for his gear, bedroll, and new duds packed in a valise. He replaced his gentleman's clothes with his travel outfit of canvas britches, linen shirt, leather vest, duster and hat. His Colt in the holster at his left hip, butt forward, and his Winchester Yellowboy in hand, and with a last glance around the room, exited with arms full and eagerness showing on his face. He paid his bill, walked out on the boardwalk and looked at the rising sun at the end of the valley, just showing itself through the notch between the hills, and stepped off to the livery.

The big dog Blue was happy to see Cord, shaking his tail so much it shook his entire rear end, and the grulla stallion turned around in the stall, lifting his head over the gate and letting a low whicker come from his chest. Cord was certain the stallion was smiling at him and he reached out to stroke the nose of Kwitcher. Even the pack mule moved his ears back and forth in greeting of the man.

With packs loaded with the panniers and parfleche that included the valise of his new duds, he geared up the pack mule, saddled Kwitcher, and was soon on the trail from town. He had stopped by the newspaper office, picked up an early map of the area and started his exploratory tour of the gold fields. He had heard the gang talk about Eureka Gulch, but he knew that was west of Central City, and Russel gulch was south, but Chase Gulch paralleled the road from Central City, just north of the long ridge that separated the two, and he started with that. When he rode north from Black Hawk, he rounded the point of the long ridge that rose high above both Black Hawk and Central City.

For placer mining, there had to be water, and the little creek that carved its way through Chase Gulch was ample for what the prospectors would need, but little else. As he followed the stream bed, he saw the murky water that told of activity upstream and it was just a short distance to the first active placer claim. A small cabin sat back from the stream, at the edge of the trees on the south side of the creek. The hillside above still held good timber, although there were many stumps on the lower reaches, signs of trees cut to make cabins, sluice boxes, and more.

Two men were busy at their claim, a long sluice with rock piles on both sides, showed considerable work. The stream had been cut with a narrow feeder ditch bringing water to the upper end of the sluice where the dirt was added to allow the water to wash it through the riffles where any gold would be trapped. One of the men stood with rifle in hand, watching as Cord rode past. Cord waved at the man, received a nod in return, and Cord was pleased to see the man keep watch until he was well past their claim. Cord reined up, turned in his saddle to look back and saw the second man replace his rifle with a shovel and join his partner.

And so it went as Cord rode west up the gulch, although a few of the claims had just one man, that man was cautious and always had a rifle within reach. None of the men were friendly and all looked suspiciously at Cord, for it was obvious he was not a prospector with no shovels, pans, or any other gear for prospecting showing on the packs. But this was just the first of several gulches he would visit, and knowing people, the further from town he got, most men were less cautious, thinking themselves safe from the possibility of attack since they were well away from town, though that just made them more vulnerable, but men with their minds on riches and gold, often let their good judgment lapse.

17

CONFRONTATION

The upper end of Chase Gulch opened to a swale of a valley some were calling Quartz valley though there was no visible quartz. A low saddle to the north beckoned Cord and he rode over the empty crossing and after taking a faint game trail through the black timber, he dropped into the valley of North Clear Creek, what was also called Missouri Canyon because of the confluence of the Missouri Creek. The south face of Missouri Canyon held sheer granite cliffs where a shoulder of the hills pushed into the canyon at the confluence of the two streams. Cord pushed into the canyon with the smaller Missouri Creek, saw only a couple claims, neither appearing too prosperous, and he turned back to ride to the west on North Clear Creek. There were a few prospect holes that dotted the hills, but until the north hills lay back with their easy slopes, there were few working claims.

Yet once the valley opened up, the claims, all working, were side by side and all were placer claims.

Cord took a trail that climbed the face of a round knobbed butte on the north side, offering him a better view of the valley of North Clear Creek to the west. As far as he could see, until the creek bent around the nose of a butte on the north side, the creek was lined with claims. He grinned to himself, thinking of the gang and what they would encounter. They had a habit of hitting the isolated claims where they met with little resistance and no witnesses. But here, if they attacked one claim, they would probably have to fight them all, and that would definitely put the odds in favor of the prospectors. Satisfied, he nudged Kwitcher back to the trail to turn toward town. He spotted a sign at the confluence of the creeks and the fork in the road that pointed to the Missouri Creek road which read *Rollinsville 10 miles.*

He dug out the crude map he picked up this morning and looked it over, glanced around the area, and decided to go north up Missouri Creek. His plan was to cross over to another draw or gulch that would take him back south to Black Hawk. The road was a crude wagon road that showed little use, and Cord guessed the claims up this draw were less than profitable. He looked at the hillsides that were freckled with juniper and ponderosa, but heavy with rocky abutments and escarpments showing the mountains to be more granite than any promising formations that might yield gold.

He had ridden just a short distance when the road and the creek parted company, with the creek coming from rougher terrain that forbid any kind of wagon travel and a quick look showed no prospect holes and probably no active claims. Cord rode a little further, the road split, he took the east fork, climbing up out of the deeper draw onto the open shoulders of a round knobbed butte. The road petered out and Cord kept to the east, believing the game trail he now followed would drop into the next valley. Once off the knob, he turned back to the south and followed another poor excuse for a road that according to his map, would bring him back to Black Hawk.

———

HE STABLED Kwitcher beside the mule and the long-eared beast acted like he was glad to see Kwitcher. Blue had gone on the ride with Cord and was not happy that he had to stay with the horse and mule instead of going to the hotel with Cord, but Cord knelt down, fed the dog some jerky and stroked his neck a little, always talking to him, then rose to return to the hotel. He was climbing the stairs with his back to the front desk when he heard a growl, "You! I'm gonna kill you!"

He turned to see Jerry Malcolm glaring at him,

his pistol in hand and ready to shoot. Cord threw himself to the side as he grabbed his Colt, just as Malcolm fired. The bullet tore into the step beside him and Cord lifted his Colt and fired. The big pistol roared and bucked, spitting flame, lead and smoke, and Cord saw the bullet blossom red on the black vest that covered Malcolm's chest. The man spun to the side, brought his pistol to bear, but Cord's second bullet was already on its way and it tore at the pocket watch and chain at Malcolm's side, driving the man back and tripping over his own feet to fall on his back, but he was not dead. Cord launched himself off the stairs and thundered toward Malcolm, who was struggling to lift his Remington pistol, cocking the hammer as he fought, but when he saw Cord standing over him, he spat blood and growled, "You...you..." then choked on his own blood, fell back onto the floor, sightless eyes staring at the ceiling.

Gunsmoke hung low in the lobby of the hotel and silence froze everyone that stared. Cord knelt beside Malcolm, looked at him and stood, kicked the pistol to the side and looked at the clerk who stood staring from behind the counter. Cord said, "You might wanna send for the sheriff."

Cord holstered his pistol, leaned back against the counter and withdrew the list from his pocket. He looked at the clerk, "Got a pencil?"

The clerk nodded, his mouth still open, and handed Cord the pencil. Cord marked off the name of Jerry Malcolm from his list. Looked down at the body, pocketed the list and lifted his eyes as the sheriff pushed open the door. He was an average sized man, just shy of six feet, a little lean, with a holstered pistol on his right hip, a badge on the chest of his black vest, a long sleeved faded grey shirt tucked into black pin stripe trousers. Scuffed boots that had at one time been black, showed considerable wear. The sheriff pushed back a tall crowned black hat to show a receding hairline with hair that was a little thinner than his handlebar moustache. The rest of his face had not been real close to a razor lately, but his black piercing eyes brokered no argument as he glared at Cord. "You do this?"

Cord nodded but did not answer.

"Why?"

"Seemed like the thing to do."

The clerk leaned over the counter, "I saw it all sheriff! That man," pointing at the body on the floor, "hollered at this'n as he was goin' up the stairs an' had his back to him," pointing again to the body. "He said, 'I'm gonna kill you!' And he was ready to shoot, but this'n turned,drew his pistol and fired just 'fore he did. An' I think that'n," pointing again to the body, "fired 'bout the same time, but he hit the rail yonder," pointing to the rail at the side of the stairs. "Then he," nodding to Cord, "fired again and that'n fell, but was still tryin' to shoot, but..." he shrugged, glancing from the sheriff to Cord.

The sheriff looked at Cord, "That right?"

Cord nodded again.

"You know him?"

"Didn't *know* him, but I knew who he was - former Jayhawker outta Missouri. He and his friends been hittin' claims, killin' prospectors, taking their money an' such."

"If you knew that, why didn't you tell me?"

"Tried, but you were gone."

"Humphhhh," grunted the sheriff, looking from Cord to the body and back. "Don'tchu leave town. I wanna talk to you. What's your name?"

"Cordell Beckett."

The sheriff nodded, continued, "Come to my office tomorrow and we'll talk 'bout this." The sheriff turned away from Cord, motioned to the clerk and told him, "Get some others and get this," motioning to the body, "outta here. Take him o'er to the under- taker, Smith."

Instead of waiting till morning, Cord followed the sheriff to his office and the sheriff motioned him to a chair, went to the stove and shook the coffee pot, only to be disappointed. He turned to Cord, "So, you often go from town to town shootin' people?"

"Only when they're shootin' at me," responded Cord, taking a seat in the chair in front of the sher- iff's desk.

He doffed his hat, sat it on the floor beside him, ran his fingers through his hair and looked up at the sheriff as the sheriff growled, "You said a lot about that man and his doin's. You been followin' him or sumpin'?"

"Somethin'."

"Now that he's dead, you done?"

"Nope. His friends will continue doin'."

"You plannin' on shootin' them too?" queried the sheriff, clasping his hands over his chest as he leaned back in his chair. He was intentionally giving Cord the impression that he was an easy-going, laid-back man that was not to be feared. But Cord had judged him to be a right savvy man that was very good at his job, and it would be dangerous to cross him.

"I don't *plan* on shootin' anybody, but I do get a little uncomfortable when they shoot at me."

"So, why shouldn't I just put you in a cell back there and not have to worry about you?"

Cord let a slow grin split his face as he reached into his vest pocket and brought out the deputy marshal badge, and held it out for the sheriff to see.

"Federal Marshal?"

Cord nodded, replaced the badge, and looked at the sheriff as he squirmed a little in his chair, leaned forward with elbows on his desk and scowled at Cord. "Why ain'tchu wearin' that on your vest?"

"People like to talk, and the badge discourages conversation. I like to listen, learn more thataway."

"So, now what'cha gonna do? 'Bout them others I mean."

"Watch, listen..." Cord shrugged.

"An' shoot?"

"Only if I have to."

"Them others, how many?"

"Four, five."

"Think they'll do anything?"

"That's what I want to find out. They were talking together, and I heard a little, sounds like they will try what they've done elsewhere – go after the prospectors at small claims, steal their gold, jump their claim, not to work, but to sell. I'm headin' out to Chase Gulch, camp out in the trees an' watch for 'em. Hopefully stop 'em 'fore they do any killin'."

The sheriff stood, looked at Cord, "All right, just tell me what's goin' on as you can, and...try to keep from killin' ever one."

Cord nodded, stood and replaced his hat, shook hands with the sheriff, and left.

18

CHASE GULCH

Rather than wait for morning, Cord gathered his gear from his room, paid his bill and went to the livery. The liveryman had a room in the building and grumbled considerably when Cord banged on the door to tell him he was leaving. As Cord rode from the town, he stood in his stirrups, breathing deep of the cool night air. There was no dust or any other unusual smells in the clear air and Cord sat back, letting Kwitcher have his head. Cord looked to the sky, the moon was waxing full and was just over half, while the clear sky was decked with stars that reveled in their black velvet canopy. He heard the call of a lonesome coyote that went unanswered, the rattling of the cicadas, and the occasional chirp of the nightbirds. High above a wide-winged eagle coasted on the updrafts, his white canopied head searching for prey as he let an occasional chirping sound to tell of his hunt.

He took the same road he traveled earlier that morning, believing the most likely place the outlaws would strike would be the upper end of Chase Gulch, before the valley opened and the working claims were more abundant. It was the way of the outlaws to strike solitary or isolated claims where there were fewer men and the deeds of the outlaws would not be witnessed. He remembered a possible campsite just past the first bend where the trail bent around the point of rocks. There were several claims in the area and none close to the others. It was just around the granite cliff face where a shoulder offered some quakies and grass that would make a good camp and far enough above the valley floor to not be suspect.

He made his camp by moonlight, choosing a spot for his cookfire at the edge of the aspen and under a big ponderosa where any smoke would be dissipated by the branches and the fire would not be visible from the creek bottom. He rolled out his blankets on the far side of ponderosa, picketed Kwitcher and the mule at the edge of the aspen, and with Blue at his side, turned in for the night.

He was up before first light, savoring the quiet of the early morning with the only sounds those of whispers of the wind through the fluttering leaves of the aspen. He rolled his blankets, tucked them away with the packs, and kindled a little fire for some coffee. As he busied himself, he decided some sourdough biscuits would be good and he set about making a batch. With the dutch oven greased with some bacon, he placed the biscuits in to cover the bottom rack that kept them off the cast iron, replaced the lid and dragged some coals from the edge of the fire, placed the dutch oven on the coals, and shoveled more on top of the lid. He put some bacon in the frying pan, noticing the coffee pot was dancing and put some coffee in the water, replaced the lid and sat it on the rock beside the fire. He sat cross-legged as he maneuvered the frying pan and the bacon, enjoying the time of solitude as Blue nudged his side and lay down beside him, staring at the frying pan with big sad eyes that pleaded for a share.

WITH HIS SPENCER hanging by the sling over his shoulder, the binoculars in the case hanging from the other shoulder, a pocketful of ammunition for the Spencer and the last cup of steaming coffee in hand, Cord worked his way to the escarpment that would be his lookout point to watch over the claims in the valley below. He stood behind the rocks, slipped the Spencer with it long telescopic sight from his shoulder and stood it beside a rock, withdrew the binoculars from the case and sat his coffee near where he would stretch out for his watch. A glance over his right shoulder showing the shadowy silhouette of the mountains made darker by the slow rising sun that was beginning to paint the eastern sky in muted shades of orange and splashing color off the bottoms of the few remaining clouds. It was a cool morning, and the breeze was just enough to keep things comfortable and mask the little sounds of the typical morning.

Cord stretched out, lifted the binoculars and could see very little in the shadowy bottom of the valley, he again turned for another look and a guesstimate as to the rising of the sun, and heard the muted clatter of hoofbeats coming from around the point of the butte. He was just west of the point of rocks, and the riders had passed the bend that marked Chase Gulch. Cord was surprised, most outlaws were not ambitious enough to make an early start for anything but a getaway, and he thought this might be a group of miners or others rather than outlaws.

Their forms were just darker shadows with the slow rising sun behind them, but they were walking their horses, either to bid their time or to make as little noise as possible to keep from alarming the prospectors. Cord lowered the binoculars, squinting to make them out, but the sun was not cooperating, and the men had the early morning light at their back. There were six riders, lined out two by two, almost in a military formation. Cord frowned, knowing the only experience these men had was to run *from* the regular military, their work as Jayhawkers often put them at odds with the military - making them fugitives. Cord continued to watch the riders with his binoculars, trying to identify them but the limited light prevented recognition. They passed the first claim after the bend, moving past without slowing.

The scattered trees on the far side stretched shadows across the rocky face of the steep hillside. On the near side, many of the trees had been sacrificed for sluices, cabins, and more, but there were still some of the aspen and cottonwoods near the little creek, the miners choosing the pines for their straight trunks for wood, leaving the softer wood of the aspen and cottonwoods with their knotty trunks. Cord could easily follow the riders with his field glasses and frowned as he looked at the rider on the far side of the second pair. From what he could see, it appeared that rider had hands tied behind his back, the heavy coat hung loosely on his frame, and the floppy hat covered his face that hung, chin almost on his chest. As he watched, the riders moved to the edge of the road, dropping off to the little creek and the diggings of a claim. Two men stood back in the trees and as the riders approached, the men lifted rifles and spoke, although Cord could not hear the conversation. The leader of the riders, a big man, leaned forward, talking and gesticulating, often motioning back toward the bound rider.

As Cord watched, he saw the man beside the bound hostage, lifted his pistol and pointed it at the head of the hostage. Some shouts rose and Cord lifted his Spencer, and sighted it on the holder of the hostage, the dim light of early morning making it difficult to get a good sight with the telescope, but Cord centered the cross-hairs on the man's upper chest. Suddenly there were shouts and gunfire, the horses jerking and side-stepping, but Cord kept his sight on the man with the pistol and as he turned to face the hostage, Cord took a quick breath, slowly squeezing the trigger and the big Spencer bucked, roared and spat smoke and fire, the bullet striking the man at the base of his throat and plowing through his chest to shatter his backbone, driving him off his saddle and onto the ground. Cord knew the bullet would get there before the sound and the surprise would be as much of a shock as any shooting or screaming.

Cord quickly scanned the other riders, saw an empty saddle behind the hostage, a man on the ground lifting his pistol toward the hostage, and Cord fired again, the bullet driving into the top of the man's shoulder, and plowing through his chest to exit out his lower side above his pelvis, crumbling the man in a heap at the side of his horse.

Cord's second shot got the attention of the other three riders who were looking into the trees above the creek and the claim, moving around, but those men only had their pistols drawn and smoking, as they moved around, grabbing reins of their mounts and trying to find the shooter that had taken two of their companions and was hiding in the trees. The men fired random shots into the trees, but without knowing where the shooter, Cord, was, the shots were futile. They grabbed their mounts and swung aboard, laying low on the saddles and jerked the horses around to take to the road and head back toward town. The last rider thought to grab the reins of the hostage's horse, but a shout from the others caused him to drop low on his saddle and follow them, leaving the hostage, with hands still bound behind his back, on a skittish horse, as he tried to control the animal with knee pressure and heels. By leaning forward, talking to the horse, the horse settled down and the rider slid from the saddle to drop to his feet, leaning back against the horse.

Cord walked from the trees, moved past the cabin and stepped out beside the two men that had confronted the outlaws, only to see one bloodied and dead, the second man, also bloodied, lying on his side looking with frightened eyes at Cord. Cord spoke, "Easy now, I'm a friend. Let me see what I can do, but first, let me get that other'n that's tied," nodding to the far edge of the stream where the former hostage stood, leaning against his horse and glaring at Cord and the two downed men. Cord leaned his rifle against a skinny aspen, waded across the creek and went to the bound man and said, "Turn around, let me get that off your arms," motioning to the bonds.

Cord glanced at the hostage, saw the neckerchief around the face and covering his mouth and he reached up to untie the neckerchief, dropped it, and reached for the rope around the wrists. He paused as he noticed the wrists were white and small, he glanced to the neck and saw smooth white skin. He quickly loosed the bonds and the hands of the former hostage came up quickly, pulling off the hat and releasing a stack of hair that shook out and showed it to be a little more than shoulder length. Cord stepped back, watching, and realized the hostage was a woman, and it was easy to see, she was a beauty. Cord stammered, "Uh, you're a woman!"

The woman glared at him, turned toward the downed men and quickly crossed the creek and went to the men. She saw the first man was dead, sightless eyes staring at the sky, blood pooling around his body. She turned to the second man and said, "Tommy! Tommy! How bad is it?"

The man called Tommy just grunted, struggling to breathe, and hunkered over. She moved closer, looked to his side and chest, glanced around and pulled her coat off, folded it to make a pillow and lay him back. Cord spoke from behind her, "You know if there's anything to use for bandages hereabouts?"

She pointed to the crude cabin, "There, in the pack in the back."

Cord nodded and trotted to the cabin, pushed inside, saw some packs and went to them. The second pack yielded the bundle of rags and more that could be used as bandages and he quickly returned to the side of the woman, handing off the stack. She glanced at him, then quickly started sorting the bandages, and began tending to the wounded man.

When she finished tending the wounds, she looked about and Cord handed her a blanket. She covered the wounded man and stood, stepped back and turned to look at Cord. "Who're you?"

Cord let a slow grin split his face and said, "I'm Cordell Beckett, and you?"

"I'm Tabitha Townsend." She paused, cocked her head to the side, motioned to the two men, "That's Thomas Townsend, and that one is Timothy. They're my brothers."

Cord slowly lifted his head, nodding, and glanced at Tommy who appeared to be sleeping or unconscious. Cord nodded to the man, "Think he's gonna be all right?"

Tabitha breathed deeply, looked at her brother, "Hope so. Dunno." She turned back to Cord, "I take it you're the one that shot from the trees?"

Cord nodded, looked at Tabitha, "Got a shovel handy? Got some buryin' to do."

Tabitha dropped her eyes, slowly shaking her head, struggling with her emotions, turned slightly and pointed to the side of the cabin. Cord nodded and started toward the cabin, he glanced back at the woman as she started into the cabin. It was a bit unusual to see a lone woman in this country, let alone a woman in man's britches and more, although it was done out of necessity, for this was a land for men, tough men, and it was hard on women. But she was a good looking woman and she looked better in those britches than any man, thought Cord, chuckling to himself. He dug the grave between the cabin and the trees, and went about three to four feet deep, even though the ground was hard and rocky. When it was ready, he walked around in front of the cabin and found Tabitha sitting on the stoop of the front door, her face showing trails of tears and her red eyes showing sorrow. He asked, "You want me to wrap his body in a blanket or...?"

She nodded, stood and went into the cabin to fetch a blanket. Cord accepted it, went to the body, wrapped it in the blanket and struggled to carry the body to the grave, but made it and lowered it as carefully and respectfully as possible. He stood, saw the woman across the grave and he reached into his duster to pull out his Bible.

He began to read Psalm 23:4 *"Yea though I walk through the valley of the shadow of death, I will fear no evil: for thou art with me; thy rod and thy staff they comfort me. Thou preparest a table before me in the presence of mine enemies: thou anointest my head with oil: my cup runneth over. Surely goodness and mercy shall follow me all the days of my life: and I will dwell in the house of the Lord forever."*

He looked at the woman who was sobbing softly into her handkerchief and he began to pray, "Our Father in Heaven, we come to you with heavy hearts and ask you for your grace. This man died needlessly, and he leaves family behind. We ask for your understanding, protection, and provision as we go forth. We commit our brother, Timothy Townsend, to you and ask for grace and strength for his family that remains. In Jesus' name, Amen."

Tabitha looked up at Cord, "Thank you, that meant a lot."

Cord nodded, and started to turn away, "Uh, I need to take care of the vermin on the other side of the creek. But first, I'm goin' up to my camp," nodding to the trees, "and get my horse and gear. I'll be back down shortly."

Tabitha nodded, "I'll put on some coffee."

CORD HAD SPOTTED a bluff with a bit of an overhang on the far side of the creek and road. With Kwitcher doing the hard work, he dragged the two bodies to the bluff, lay them in the dip below the road and climbed up the bluff to cave in the overhang and cover the bodies. Satisfied, he looked heavenward, "Lord, I don't know nothin' 'bout those two, but they were up to no good, so you can do what you think is right." He swung back aboard the grulla and with a wave to Blue, they returned to the cabin where the mule was tethered in the shade. He tethered the grulla, started for the cabin but went to the side of the brother called Thomas, knelt down beside him and saw his breathing was raggedy, but steady. He pulled the blanket up around the man, then walked to the open door of the cabin and called out, "All right if I come in?"

"Coffee's ready," answered Tabitha.

19

RETALIATION

CORD ACCEPTED THE CUP OF STEAMING COFFEE, SAVORED the aroma, and with a glance to Tabitha, stepped outside to seat himself on a bench just outside the door but in the shade of a tall cottonwood. Tabitha joined him, sitting quietly as she watched her brother who lay in the shade a short way from the cabin. He was restless, but still unconscious, his wounds showing bloody on the bandages. She sat her coffee down, dropped her face into her hands and wept. Cord sat silently by, allowing the woman her moment of grief.

When she collected herself and sat back, she lifted the coffee cup to her lips and sat quiet for a moment. Cord asked her, "How'd it happen that you were with those men?"

She dropped her eyes, and began, "I went into town for some supplies. My brothers protested but I insisted. They can do more with the sluice than I can so I thought I could help by going for supplies. When I was in the store, two of those men saw me, waited for me outside and when I started to leave town, they grabbed me and took me to the others that were camped outside of town. They tried to use me to force my brothers to sign over the claim and give them what gold they had, but...well, Tim was always the hothead of the twins and he lifted his rifle, but the big man, I think they called him Newt, shot him, and that started it all. I thought one of my brothers shot the man beside me, but then I heard your rifle, it makes a bigger sound than my brother's, and I knew there was somebody else. Before I knew it, it was all over. I was scared they were going to take me with them, but..." she shrugged. She lifted her eyes to Cord, "I'm thankful for what you've done. If it hadn't been for you, well..." she shrugged again, and dropped her eyes.

Cord had been watching her brother while she spoke and rose from his seat, placed the coffee cup on the bench and walked over to where Tom lay, he looked down at the still form, dropped to one knee to feel for a pulse but there was none. Tommy was dead. Tabitha had followed Cord and knelt beside him, looked from Cord to her brother and dropped her face into her hands and let the tears flow. Cord lay his arm gently over her shoulders and pulled her a little closer and let her lean against him as she wept.

She pulled away, struggled to her feet and Cord

stood beside her. He walked with her into the cabin, waited as she went to one of the bunks and lay down, turning her face to the wall. Cord went outside and began digging the second grave. When he finished, he wrapped the body in a blanket, and lowered it into the grave beside the brother. It was mid-day when he finished, and he went to the creek to clean up and wash off. He heard riders coming and he quickly retreated to the trees, snatching up his Spencer as he did, then turned to watch the road to see who was coming up the road.

Three men, who looked every bit the prospector, were riding together, horses at a walk, but Cord noticed they were looking about and all three had rifles across the pommels of their saddles. As they neared the Townsend claim, they turned down to the creek and pushed across to come toward the cabin. Cord called from the trees, "Hold it right there!"

The men stopped, their hands gripping the stocks of their rifles tightly as they craned to look around. One of the men called out, "We're looking for the Townsend boys, are they around?"

"They're around. Back here by the cabin. Just buried 'em both! What's your business?"

"Buried!? What happened?" asked the man in front.

"Claim jumpers!"

"You one of 'em?"

"Nope, I buried two of 'em on the other side of the road. The others ran off!"

"What about the girl? Tabitha, she around?"

"She's inside, she's all right."

"Could you come out where we can talk without yellin'?"

Cord moved from behind the tree, carried the Spencer out to stand it against a tree and stood before the men.

"Can you tell us what happened? We've been afraid of somethin' like this. We've got claims further up the creek," explained the man.

Cord motioned for them to step down, and after slipping their rifles into their scabbards, the three swung down and walked into the shade before Cord. One of the men spotted the graves, shook his head, "Hate to see that. They had a good start here." He looked up at Cord, extended his hand, "I'm Owen Jenks, this here's," motioning to the man on his left, "Steve Locke, and the other'n there is Alfred Marshal."

Cord shook hands as he responded, "I'm Cordell Beckett."

Alfred spoke up, "Musta happened kinda early. How'd you happen by?"

"I was camped up yonder," nodding to the tree behind him and above the cabin, "heard 'em comin' just as I was fixin' my coffee. Didn't like the looks of 'em, saw one was tied and gagged. So...I interfered."

"Tied and gagged?" asked Steve, frowning.

"The woman, Tabitha. Din't know it was a woman at first, but when the shootin' started, I joined in, but they'd already cut loose on the brothers."

"Wished we'd a know'd about it 'fore this so we coulda been a little more prepared. We been thinkin' somethin' like this was gonna happen. Oh, there's been a few scrapes and such, one fella was kilt an' his claim jumped, but that was a while back. If we'd only knowed..."

"I came this way yesterday, but everybody was so jumpy, it din't look too healthy to stop an' talk, me bein' a stranger an' all."

"You knew about it 'fore it happened?"

"Suspected. Heard some talk, came to look things over and tell, but when a stranger approaches a claim..." he shrugged.

"Well, yeah. But you can see why," responded Owen.

Cord nodded, "Ummhmm. But now you might wanna warn any others you meet. There were five of 'em in this bunch, three got away. But there were others with 'em in the tavern. I think they might try again, maybe not up this gulch, but somewhere near."

Owen nodded, looked at his friends who were nodding in agreement, then Owen turned his attention back to Cord, "You gonna be around?"

"Dunno, might stick around to help Tabitha if she wants, but if not, I'll mosey..."

"It'd be good to have you on our side," suggested Alfred, glancing to his friends who nodded their agreement. The men mounted and turned away, giving a wave over their shoulder as they pushed across the creek. Cord returned to the bench, picked up his coffee cup and went back inside for a refill. Tabitha rolled over, sat up on the edge of the bunk and asked, "Could you pour me another cup?"

"Sure," answered Cord and did as he had been bidden.

She ran her fingers through her hair, looked at Cord as he came near with the coffee and she smiled, "I must look a sight!" trying to chuckle at herself.

Cord grinned, "Oh, you're a sight alright, but a mighty pretty sight." He gave her a wide smile, backed away and seated himself at the little table facing her. He thought to himself, she *was* a pretty sight. Dark brown hair that tumbled over her shoulders, big blue eyes that seemed to sparkle with mischief even in the midst of her grief, and there was no question about her womanly features as she filled out those men's clothes like nothing he had ever seen before. He shook his head slightly at his own thoughts, reached for the coffee cup to change his focus, and asked, "So, I know you haven't had time to think about it, but any idea what you're gonna do now?"

She looked at him with a stare of incredulity and with a frown, answered, "Why, work the claim, of course! It's just as much mine as it was theirs!"

"You know what you're doin'?"

"Of course. I worked right alongside them from

the start!" She paused, lowered her voice and looked at the floor, "Nothin' else I can do."

"Oh, I don't know. You could probably sell the claim, get some money toward doin' somethin' else, maybe go back to wherever your home was before."

"Can't. Our folks were kilt at Lawrence by the Jayhawkers."

Cord had been looking at his coffee as he listened to Tabitha, but that caught his attention and his eyes flared and he looked up, "When was that?"

"In late summer, '63."

"And the boys were there?"

"The whole family was, but Pa made me and the twins hide out in the orchard. We had us a hideout where we played when we was little. But when that happened, my brothers were fifteen and I was thirteen. They never found us, but when we went back, the house was burnt, so was the barn, but we made out. There was a storehouse we used for a while, we tried to rebuild the house, but sold out for what we could get and the boys joined up. I stayed with a maiden aunt, my mother's sister, until they come home after the war. Then we talked about it, and came west lookin' for gold."

Cord dropped his eyes, lifted his head and looked about, then glanced at Tabitha, "Those men that tried to jump your claim were Jayhawkers."

Tabitha sat up, frowning and glaring at Cord, "How'd you know that?"

"I've been after 'em ever since they hit our family's farm in Missouri. That was three years ago now. There were about fifteen, sixteen of 'em. Whittled 'em down some, still after the others."

"Is that why you were up yonder in the trees?"

"Ummhmm. Their leader's a fella name of Newt Morrison. There's others, they've recruited a few as they go, but of the original there's only 'bout four of 'em left."

"You still after 'em?"

Cord slowly nodded his head, sipped some coffee and looked back to Tabitha, knowing what was coming.

"I wanna go with you! Let me go with you! I owe 'em!" she growled, glaring at Cord.

"I don't know if this bunch is the same as those that hit Lawrence," stated Cord.

"They're Jayhawkers, ain't they!" she growled, standing and glaring at Cord.

He grinned, nodded, and lifted his cup for a refill.

20

COMPANY

Tabitha had insisted that Cord call her Tabby, "It's what my brothers always called me since I was big 'nuff to know what they was sayin'. Can't hardly answer to anything else." He grinned at the thought as he rolled from his blankets. She had given him a lot to think about, but he was not anxious to take on another traveling companion, much less one that would want to be involved in everything he was about. But, he had to admit, she was quite fetching and there was something special about her that just seemed right. He could not explain it, but maybe it was that she was comfortable to be around. He chuckled as he rolled his blankets, looking at the dim light of early morning as it made dark shadows of the hills beyond the creek. He listened to the chuckling of the creek waters, the chirps of early rising birds, and even the chatter of an angry squirrel high above in the big cottonwood.

He went to a knob of rocks that jutted from the cottonwoods above the creek, and with Bible in hand, he began talking to his best friend of the morning as he muttered his prayer for the day. His thoughts kept returning to the woman and if he should have her with him. What he was about was not what one could call safe traveling, but he was bound to bring the rest of the Jayhawkers and their recruits to some form of justice. But that was also what she wanted. Yet, as he thought about her, knowing she was all alone, although she did seem to be able to take care of herself, he knew he could not leave her behind. He finished his prayers, and just as he said, "Amen," he heard horses on the road.

He dropped off the rocks, returned to the trees beside the cabin, and took up his Winchester, looked to the road and saw two riders coming from up the draw, but they turned from the road as if to cross the creek and come to the cabin. The sun was stretching the shadows and sliding its gold down the hillsides as they neared. They turned from the road to cross the creek. Cord stepped from beside the cabin, rifle cradled in his arms as he recognized the riders as two of the men that stopped by yesterday. They waved and reined up, leaning forward on their pommels as the one called Owen Jenks greeted, "Mornin'. Is Miss Townsend about?"

Cord heard movement from behind him as the door opened and a voice answered, "I'm about. What'chu need so early in the mornin'?"

Jenks motioned about stepping down and she answered, "Step down, I've got coffee on and welcome." She looked at Cord as he turned and said softly, "Please come inside with us. I don't want to be alone."

Cord nodded and followed Tabby through the door, knowing the two men were close behind. Tabby motioned to the table and the two chairs and two stools and the men seated themselves as she poured the coffee and seated herself beside Cord. Jenks took a sip, nodded, and exclaimed, "Good coffee!"

Tabby replied, "Thanks, now..." and nodded for the two men to state their business.

"Well, Miss Townsend, knowing what happened, you know, 'bout your brothers an' all, we got to thinkin'. Me'n Steve here's partners on our claim, and we thought you might be wantin' to sell this claim, and if so, we'd be interested."

"Well, I had thought about working it, but..." she glanced to Cord, "I've also thought about leaving. I have some other business to tend to."

The three talked some more, discussing the claim, possible payment and more and Cord rose, left the table and stood in the doorway, watching the road and the rising of the sun, but listening to the discussion. When it paused, Tabby rose and came behind him, touched his shoulder and asked, "Could we talk, outside, please?"

Cord nodded, stepped outside and walked away

from the cabin to a shady spot near where the horse
and mule were picketed. Blue stayed at his side and
Cord turned to face the woman. She began with,
"Have you thought any more about me coming with
you, you know, in the hunt for the Jayhawkers?"

"I have, but Tabby, it can get dangerous and I
would not want to see you hurt. I had a woman that
was with me early on, and they killed her. I just can't
allow that."

"I will take any risk, but I will also do whatever
you want. Please...I can't stay here and what these
men are offering, and with what I have from my
brother's work on the claim, it would be a good
stake, for the both of us."

Cord faced her, gently took her hands in his and
drew her close, "We'll have to get you ready, I mean
ready to fight. Can you use a rifle or a pistol?"

She smiled, "I've been using both a rifle and a
pistol since I was big enough to keep up with my
brothers. Whenever they went hunting, I was right
there with them. I could out shoot them most of the
time."

He grinned, "Do you *have* a pistol or rifle?"

"I have both, and more. My brothers had rifles
and pistols, and so do I." She smiled and added, "I
have a custom Baby Dragoon in .36 caliber converted
for metallic cartridges! And I have a rifle, just like the
one you had with you just a moment ago, a
Winchester Yellow Boy in .44 caliber!"

Cord was surprised to hear her talk about the

weapons, a subject most women would avoid, and the way she talked about them showed she was proud of what she had and was confident in her use of them. He dropped his eyes, lifted them to look hard at her, "So, I guess it's up to you. If you want to sell and leave this all behind and go who knows where after this bunch, then I guess..." he shrugged, letting a slow grin split his face.

She smiled, quickly rose to her toes, and kissed him on the cheek before she turned away to trot back into the house before he could change his mind. Cord chuckled as he watched, shaking his head, thinking. *Either I'm the biggest fool around or I just agreed to something that will probably get me killed.*

———

TABBY WAS BETTER OUTFITTED than Cord expected. She and her brothers had horses in a corral that allowed them access to the creek and a lean-to shed for cover. When she led her horse out, Cord had to do a double take. It was a high-stepping sorrel mare with a blaze face, four stockings, and flaxen mane and tail. She was a beautiful animal and well built at just shy of fifteen hands, short back, broad chest and a bit of an arch to her neck. Tabby grinned as she watched Cord's reaction, chuckling as she tied the horse to the rail fence and began saddling the animal with confidence. Refusing any help from Cord, she soon had the horse saddled, her saddlebags filled with necessities, her rifle in the scabbard under the right fender, the saddle bags secured behind the cantle and her bedroll with a change of clothes tied on behind the cantle. She led the mare to the cabin, tied her off next to Kwitcher, who was tossing his head and moving closer to get acquainted.

Cord was sitting on the stoop of the cabin, nursing a cup of hot coffee and Tabby smiled and asked, "Where's mine?" pointing to the coffee.

Cord rose, grinned, "Yes ma'am, I'll fetch you a cup, right away ma'am!" and chuckled as he turned into the cabin. He quickly returned with a cup of steaming java for Tabby who had seated herself on the stoop, leaving room for him beside her. She was wearing rust colored canvas trousers, an ivory-colored twill shirt, and a rough-out leather chore coat, all under a narrow-brimmed felt hat. With her long hair hanging over her shoulders and the way she filled out the clothes, there was no mistaking she was a woman. But Cord was thinking he would rather she had more of a look that would make her pass for a man by anyone that was not close.

He sipped on his coffee and asked, "You've got a change of clothes in your bedroll?"

She nodded, smiling, "Yes, and they're much the same as this. My brothers did not want me looking too much like a woman, you know, to attract attention."

"I agree. We might pick you up a duster like I wear. It'll cover a little more," he grinned, a little embarrassed at himself and what he was saying, "and it'll keep you dry in the rain an' such." He sipped his coffee to hide his embarrassment, but she noticed and giggled, nudging him with her shoulder.

"So, what now?" asked Tabby, her elbows on her knees as she sat beside Cord.

"We'll go back into town, look around a bit, maybe go to the store and get you that duster and any other supplies we might need. I don't think the Jayhawkers will be coming back up this way, but they might have hit some other claims, and if so, there'll be word about it, and then we'll decide what we'll be doing, or where we'll go."

"Good. I'd like to go to the bank, swap some dust for actual money."

"We can do that. But it's best not to do too much at once. People talk and the word could get around that you're carrying a bit of money which might be tempting to the wrong people."

"Well, if we're gonna be travelin' about, I don't want to leave it behind, even in a bank. But it's not like I'm rich or anything. It's just enough to, well, keep goin' a while."

Cord nodded, sat his coffee cup down and said, "Let's go back in the trees here. I want to see how you handle your weapons. We'll do a little target practice."

Tabby grinned, rose, and went to her saddle and retrieved the rifle. She wore her pistol on her hip in much the same way as Cord, butt forward, left hip.

They walked into the trees, far enough away from the cabin and the horses as to not cause alarm, and Cord picked up a couple of big pine cones dropped from a tall ponderosa and sat them on a grey log that was in a bit of an open clearing with ample sunlight.

He walked back to her side, looked back at the cones that were a good twenty-five yards away, and looked at her as she held the rifle cradled in her arms and said, "One shot, take the cone on the right."

She smiled, turned a little sideways with her left side toward the target, lifted the rifle, sighted, took a breath and let it out some, and squeezed off her shot. The rifle bucked and spat a bullet that shattered the cone.

He grinned, "Good shooting. Now try the next one with the pistol."

She handed him the rifle, turned to face Cord with her right side to the log, lifted the pistol one handed, took a quick aim and dropped the hammer. The cone exploded when the .36 caliber slug smashed into it. She lowered the pistol, turned to look at Cord with a big smile, "Do I pass?"

"Ummhmmm, you pass. But it's different when the pine cones are shooting back!"

21

HUNT

THEY WAITED TILL MORNING TO PUT THE CLAIM BEHIND them and side by side rode into the rising sun to make the trip back to Black Hawk. Their first stop was at the general store for some supplies, ammunition, flour, bacon, beans, and other essentials. They bided their time, looking around, listening to others talking and sharing the news. Even though Black Hawk had a newspaper now, the habit of sharing the news with one another was still the preferred way to stay informed. One man had gathered most of his goods on the counter and was talking with the owner as he settled his bill, "Yeah, I guess they hit two claims, kilt the owners an' took off with their pokes an' more. By the tracks an' such, there musta been a half dozen of 'em what done it!"

"Were the claims close?" asked the clerk.

"Within' shoutin' distance, but when the shootin' started, there weren't no place to hide, bein' up Missouri Crick where there ain't much timber left, an' they din't wanna leave their claims, but it cost 'em, sho'nuff!"

"Missouri Creek, that's what, four, five miles from here?"

"Oh, at least that, prob'ly more like eight or ten."

The clerk was shaking his head, worry wrinkling his brow, as he figured up the tally on the man's goods. The clerk looked at the man, "That'll be five dollars and eighty-five cents. How far is your claim from those two that were taken?"

"Oh, mine's 'bout four miles on up the crick, but if'n I don't get more color soon, I'm quittin' it and goin' elsewhere."

As the man gathered his goods and turned away from the counter, Cord asked, "When did those claims get hit?"

"Yestiddy, just 'fore sundown."

Cord nodded and watched as the man hauled his goods outside, and soon returned for the rest. Cord found a duster that looked to be about the size for Tabitha and held it up to her, pursed his lips as he looked at it, nodded, and added it to the stack of goods on the counter. They settled their bill, loaded up their goods and went out to pack things away in the panniers and parfleche on the pack mule. As they put things away, Cord asked Tabitha, "When those men first grabbed you, did they take you anywhere? You know, before they came to the claim."

"Ummhmm, but they put a neckerchief around

my head to cover my eyes and another'n to keep me from hollerin'. But it was a cabin near the Bobtail lode. I could hear the ore carts and such, and the men were talking. After I was inside, they took off the blinders and gag, and I could see a little out the window, but it was comin' on dark but not so dark's I couldn't see the dumps outside the mine. The big tipple was high on the hill, and the cabin where we were was below the dumps. I think I've seen it before. And they had a corral for the horses and a shed for 'em too." She stepped back, cocked her head to the side and looked at Cord, "Why, what're you thinkin'?"

"While we're here in town, I'd like to get a look at that cabin, see if any of 'ems around there, maybe get an idea of their plans or..." he shrugged, tightening the cinch on the packsaddle. He turned back to Tabitha, holding the duster in one hand and said, "How 'bout you tryin' this on?"

She slipped off her rough-out chore coat and turned for Cord to help her into the duster. It was a good fit, a little loose but comfortable, and Cord was satisfied it would cover more of her womanliness. He chuckled, "Now, see if you can stack some o' that hair up in your hat, or at least put it down in your coat, turn your collar up and hide it a little."

"Why are you so concerned about me looking like a woman?"

"Because if they see two riders and one is obviously a woman, then whenever they see us again, they'll know us. But two riders that appear just like two men, they won't think much of it."

"Unless they see our horses. Ain't nobody gonna forget two riders on horses like these and draggin' a pack mule. And don't even think about it. I ain't gettin' rid of Cassi!"

Cord chuckled, "Cassi?"

"Ummhmm, short for her full name, Cassiopeia, the constellation of stars. My daddy showed me where it is and I liked the name, so..." she shrugged, smiling.

Cord was shaking his head, knowing she was right about them being remembered wherever they went, if for no other reason than the horses they rode. Both the flaxen maned sorrel filly and his grulla stallion were exceptional animals, and for anyone that appreciated fine horses, they would be remembered. "Well then, I reckon we'll just have to keep 'em outta sight!"

————

THEY RODE FROM BLACK HAWK, going back to Chase Gulch, but as soon as they rounded the point of the ridge and turned west up the gulch, Cord nudged Kwitcher to the trees, looking for a game trail that would take them to the crest of the ridge. He knew the Bobtail lode was on the south face of the ridge and believed they could get a look at the cabin below from the crest of the ridge. An old game trail showed itself and Cord let Kwitcher have his head as the narrow trail meandered across the face of the slope, always climbing higher and cutting back on itself several times. As they neared the crest and the edge of the trees, the trail straddled a slight shoulder and Cord reined up. He turned to Tabitha, "Let's tie the horses here and go the rest of the way on foot. I'm hopin' to get a look at the cabin from up here and you need to point it out for me."

She nodded, stepped down, and finding a bit of a shoulder with graze and sunlight, she tethered her mare and saw Cord doing the same with his stallion and the mule. They took their Winchesters in hand and Cord had the case with the binoculars hanging from his shoulder as they made their way to the edge of the trees just below the crest of the ridge. Cord dropped to a crouch, to continue to the ridge crest and was followed by Tabitha. They bellied down at the crest, crawled closer and stopped when Tabitha pointed and said, "There, that'n with the corral."

The weather-beaten cabin showed its age and wear, and the corral held two horses and a mule. Cord slipped the binoculars from the case and focused in on the cabin. The horses and mule stood hipshot in the corral, heads hanging, tails swatting flies, but no other life showed. Until the door of the outhouse slapped open and a man staggered from the privy, pulling his galluses over his shoulder that showed only his faded red union suit. He looked toward the cabin, shouted something at someone that was obviously in front of the cabin, and disappeared around the corner of the building.

Cord lowered the binoculars, looked at Tabitha, "Looks to be only two of 'em at the cabin now, which means the others are prob'ly out rampagin' somewhere." He handed the binoculars to Tabitha, frowned as he thought about the gang. He remembered the one called Newt as Newt Morrison, but the two that were killed at the claim did not look familiar and he did not know their names. The others that turned tail and ran included Morrison but the others were not familiar. Those that were at the table in the tavern the night before he killed Malcolm, only one other than Morrison, looked familiar and Cord thought he was James Flood. As far as the names on his list that now included some of the recruits, there were Bill Coogan, Buck Smithers, and Jose Espinoza. That would be five men, plus these two, if they were a part of the bunch. Cord's thoughts were interrupted when Tabby said, "They're comin' out!"

She handed the binoculars to Cord and he focused in on the men as they caught up their mounts and began saddling them, but Cord was surprised to see one of the men saddling the mule and the second man chose the buckskin. Neither man looked familiar, but they could have been at the table in the tavern with Morrison and he still would not recognize them, it was too dark to see any of them well. He lowered the binoculars and looked at Tabitha, "Do they look familiar to you?"

"Yes, they were in the cabin that night. There were seven men in all, and you killed two at the claim. But didn't that man say there were at least a half dozen that raided the claims up Missouri Gulch?"

"He did, but he was talking about tracks and unless he's a good woodsman and tracker, it would be easy to make a mistake as to the number. But I'm guessing the other five are up one of these gulches and probably sizing up their next claim, or already taking it."

They stayed on the ridge until the men left, but were unable to tell where they were going as they took the road into Black Hawk. On a hunch, Cord grabbed the binoculars and walked to the point of the ridge, keeping below the crest so he would not be sky lined, and to where he could see into the town as well as the mouth of Chase Gulch. This was also the road that would take them up the North Fork of Clear Creek and to Missouri Gulch. If he could see where they went, it might tell where the others might be as well. Tabitha stayed close behind, and when they came to the point of the ridge, they crouched down and Cord began scanning the valley below.

They spent a good hour watching the trails and roads leading from Black Hawk into the gulches that harbored the placer claims, but they did not see where the two men from the cabin went. Cord lowered the binoculars, looked at Tabitha, "They musta just wanted to go to town to get a drink. Maybe disappeared into one of the taverns, or..." he thought a moment. "Maybe we'll go back to town, get a room at the hotel, and see if we can find 'em in the taverns." He chuckled, "Not us, me. We'll get us a good meal, then you can stay in the hotel while I go to the taverns and see if I can find 'em, maybe hear what they're planning."

"You sound like my brothers – making me stay home while they went to the tavern," pouted Tabitha, sitting back with arms folded across her chest, a frown on her face.

Cord laughed, "Well, you and I both know that a tavern is no place for a lady."

"You're not my brother or my father, so who are you to say?" she grumbled.

Cord just grinned, stood, and said, "C'mon, let's go."

22

SEARCH

As they rode back into town, Cord spotted a saddled mule, and a big bay, tethered at the hitchrail in front of the Prospector, a popular café that catered to the working man. Beside the mule was a buckskin, and Cord knew the two men from the cabin must be having their supper in the café. He turned to Tabitha, "That's the mule and buckskin those two were riding. Let's go have supper shall we?"

As they tethered their animals at the other hitchrail, Tabby asked, "How we gonna know who they are?"

"Well, first off, if *you* recognize them. But one of 'em was purty short, and the only hair he had was on his chin, and it was grey. The other'n was tall an' skinny."

Tabby grinned, chuckling at Cord's description. They stepped up on the boardwalk, Cord opened the door for Tabby, and they entered the small dining room. There were only a half dozen tables, most with four chairs, one with six, and the one in the corner had only two chairs occupied. Cord noticed the men turn away quickly, realizing they had recognized Tabitha. He glanced to Tabby, said, "Follow my lead," and started to the table. He grabbed one of the empty chairs, and pulled it out, motioning for Tabby to be seated and he took the other one. Both men were startled and started to object until Cord pulled back his duster to show the butt of his pistol, then sat down as he said, "Well, hello fellas. Been here long?" He noticed they only had cups of coffee before them.

The bigger of the two men growled, "Nah, just got here. They ain't brought our food yet."

"Good, then we'll order and join you. That's alright, isn't it?" asked Cord, showing a grin to the men. "Sides, we got some questions for you."

The waitress was at their side and asked, "How may I help you?"

"What are our friends havin'?"

"They ordered the special, beef roast with biscuits and gravy."

"We'll have that, thank you," stated Cord, then he turned back to the men.

He glared at the two, his dark eyes slightly squinted, his nostrils flaring as he leaned forward, leaning against the table. "Now, I reckon you two have recognized the young lady here, and she recognized you two as being in the cabin the night she was taken by the Jayhawkers, and you didn't do anything to help her! I would have every right to just blow a hole in your gizzard right now," he reached toward his pistol to emphasize the remark, "but, we want to find your partners, and you're gonna tell us where they are!"

The smaller of the two, his bald head showing red and his eyes wide with fear said, "We don't know where they are! We're just glad they left! An' we couldn't do anything to help her, there was five of 'em and they took our guns!" he whined. The bigger man was nodding his agreement as he leaned back away from Cord, but fear showing in his eyes.

The second man added, "When they had her, and left the cabin with her, they said they weren't gonna hurt her. They said they was just usin' her to get the men at their claim to pay up. Said they owed money to 'em."

Cord looked from one to the other, then turned to Tabby, "So, did they do anything to help you or hurt you?"

Tabby looked from one to the other and now that she could see them better, she knew who they were, then to Cord, "That one," nodding to the bald one, "brought me a blanket, and that'n," nodding to the bigger man, "gave me a biscuit and some water. They didn't hurt me, but the others didn't either, they were just rough with me."

The little one spoke up, "I'm Curly, he's Bones. We ain't a part of that bunch. They come on our cabin 'fore we knew what they was doin' and they threatened to kill us if'n we done anythin'." He looked to Tabby, "I'se glad to see you is alright, missy."

"Did they say anything about where they were going or what they were up to?" asked Cord.

"No, no. They talked among themselves a lot and growled at us if we tried to listen. But I did hear 'em say Rollinsville and Nevada City," said Bones. "We're just glad they're gone. They ate ever'thin' we had in the cabin, that's why we're here." He reached for his coffee, looked at Cord, and said, "And if you was smart, you'd stay well away from 'em. That bunch is killers!"

Tabby said, "We know. They killed my brothers!"

"Oh, I'm sorry, missy," whined Curly, reaching out to touch Tabby's hand but she pulled away from him.

"That's what I mean," added Bones, "Ya oughta stay away from 'em, and that goes double for you missy. That's like havin' a death wish, goin' after them!"

Their meals were brought and they ate together. Bones and Curly were still a little nervous and kept glancing Cord's way, but Cord sat close to Tabby and they enjoyed the meal. Bones spoke up, "If'n you're goin' lookin' for 'em, you might wanna try Nevada

City first. There's more gold up there than in Rollinsville, and more claims. The town's purty prosperous too."

"Nevada City is back past Central City, isn't it?" asked Cord.

"Ummhmm, it's tween Eureka Gulch an' the stage road back to Idaho Springs. Most of the town's on the south facing hill above the crick. I tried my luck up there, din't get nuthin'."

THE SETTING SUN was painting the western sky as Cord and Tabby started from Black Hawk. The bold colors faded on the hillsides and shone on the faces of the two companions. Tabby smiled as she closed her eyes and lifted her face to the fading warmth of the closing day. Cord glanced to her, rocking in her saddle, a broad smile on her blushing face, her eyes closed as she leaned back just enough to capture the last bit of sunshine that struggled from behind the few clouds that offered a palette of colors for the end of day. She opened one eye to look to Cord, and said, "There's no hotel thisaway!"

"Nope," answered a grinning Cord.

"Then what're we doin'?"

"Headin' for Nevada City."

"Now? It'll be dark soon!" she declared as she leaned forward, her free hand on the pommel as she frowned at Cord.

"Ummhmm, but we'll find us a good campsite th' other side of Central City. Wanna get away from people, at least for a little while. I'm not sure those two were totally truthful, but..." he shrugged. "Sides, the fresh air is better for you than the smoke- filled hotels and rooms."

Tabby laughed, her expression agreeing with Cord, but she looked at him with her head cocked to the side and her eyes squinted just a mite as she asked, "And just what do you have in mind?"

"Me? Nothin', it's just not the proper thing for a lady to share a room in a hotel with a single gentleman."

She giggled, "Oh, so now you're a gentleman?"

Cord grinned, "Ummhmm, that's what my father taught me!"

"But, it's alright to camp out in the woods with a single man, nobody else around, and all?" she smiled coyly.

"I'm not just a single man - I'm your protector!" he stated, lifting his head and looking around with a stoic expression painting his face.

"And who's going to protect me from you?" giggled Tabby, smiling.

"Ha! The way you were shooting, the question should be, who's going to protect *me* from *you!*"

They had just cleared Black Hawk when Cord nudged Kwitcher to the trees on the south of the valley, looking for a game trail that would take them around Central City and across Spring Gulch. It was easy riding through the trees that had been thinned out considerably by the miners and others searching for tall trees to build their cabins and sluice boxes and more. They crossed the stage road in the bottom of Spring Gulch and took to the trees of the round knob that lay on the flanks of the line of hills that marched toward Bald Mountain. As they rounded the hill, the pines gave way to aspen, the shadowy form of Bald Mountain showed before the distant granite-tipped peaks that made the jagged horizon of the western mountains.

The trail took them between two prospect holes that appeared to be abandoned with weeds and seedlings sprouting on the lower edges of the dumps. As they moved past this badge of failure, they rose onto a bit of a saddle and Cord reined up, looked about in the dim light of dusk, and nodded. He looked at Tabby, "This'll do. Come daylight we can see further up the valley and get a better idea of the layout of the area."

"How do you suppose we'll find 'em?"

"Dunno, but I reckon we can talk to some of the claim owners, warn 'em, and..." he shrugged as he dropped to the ground. He took the reins of both horses and the lead from the mule, made a picket line and tethered the animals and began stripping the gear. Tabby had wandered into the trees, gathering some firewood and learning the area. Cord brushed each of the animals, talking to them as he worked, Blue lying nearby and watching. He had not seen a grinning Tabby watching him through the trees. When he finished and carried their bedrolls to the flat where she was preparing a fire ring under the wide branches of a ponderosa, she looked up at him, "You do that often?"

"Do what?"

"Talk to the horses."

"Most often my horse and dog are the only ones I have to talk to, and they like it. In this country where companions are rare, most men do it, if for no other reason but so they won't feel so alone."

"Is that how men get used to doing all the talking and not listening?"

Cord grinned, dropped the bedrolls and shook his head as he rolled out his own, watching Tabby roll hers nearby but with the fire ring between them. He returned to the packs, retrieved the coffee pot, frying pan, and the parfleche with some of the food-stuffs including the coffee. When he arranged those things near the fire, he looked up at Tabby, frowned, "Woman cook. Cook good, if no good, man spank!" he growled, giving a crude imitation of an Indian brave.

"Woman cook good. If man no like, woman shoot man, get another!" responded a grinning Tabby, her stern expression matching Cord's. They both laughed and unfolded their blankets, preparing their beds for the night. Cord had chosen the spot under the ponderosa for the thick layer of long pine needles that would make a softer bed for the night. As they stretched out, Cord had his hands clasped behind his head, looking through the branches at the moon that was just over half and waxing to full. He smiled and said, "Good night squaw!"

"Ugh!" responded Tabby, trying to stifle her giggle.

23

NEVADA CITY

CORD SAT SILENT, WATCHING THE RISING SUN PAINT THE granite tipped peaks with a fiery gold, slowly letting the paint slide down the mountains to catch the tips of the timber covered foothills that littered the terrain before the blue mountains. He sat on a big boulder that hugged the shoulder of the hill with scattered pines, spruces and firs that blanketed the hills with a deep green that contrasted with the pale greens of the aspen that grew in the gulches and draws of the foothills. It was a sight that Cord had grown to appreciate and filled him with awe of the splendor of the Creator. He took a deep breath of the cool morning air, filling his lungs with the fresh scents of pine, aspen, the occasional kinnikinnick or currant bushes.

He caught a whiff of coffee, turned back to their camp, and joined Tabby who sat grinning and

holding a steaming cup of coffee before her. As Cord
stepped close, she handed the cup to Cord and asked,
"Did you tell Him I said Hi?"

Cord frowned, "Tell who?"

"The one you were talkin' to, you know, God!"

Cord chuckled, sat down across from her and
with elbows on his knees, he said, "That's somethin'
you need to do yourself!"

"I do, but a little extra never hurts!" she giggled
as she poured herself a cup of coffee.

She took a sip, looked at Cord, "So, what do we
do today?"

"We'll break camp, go into town, look around
and see what might be happening, see if we can hear
any news of the gang of thugs that we're after,
then..." he shrugged, lifting his cup for another sip.

"Can't we just ride out and talk to the
prospectors?"

"Last time I thought about that, well, let's just
say I didn't get much of a welcome."

Tabby smiled, "Yeah, but now, you got me!" she
put one hand to the side of her face and smiled as if
she was posing for a picture.

Cord made a face, pursed his lips as he cocked his
head to the side as he looked at her, "Might work,
if'n it don't scare 'em to death!" he chuckled.

She made a face right back, looked around, and
picked up a stick and threw it at him. Cord ducked,
shook his finger at her and said, "Keep that up and I

might hafta turn you over my knee and give you a spanking!"

"Hah! Try that and you'll be sorry!" she warned, laughing.

———

THE SUN HAD FINALLY SHOWN its face over the crest of the eastern hills, bending its golden hues to show the town of Nevada City as it lay in the bottom of the valley. As was true of the other settlements in these parts, the hills were scalped of any and all timber that could be used for anything from firewood to building timbers, leaving the scattered debris littering the hillsides. On the north facing slope, a road had been carved across the face to access several prospect holes and a handful of cabins, while across the valley, there were scattered cabins, some looking sturdy, others not so much and showing sagging rooflines that threatened to give way with the next snowfall.

Stretching across the bottom of the valley, a single road was sided on both the north and south, with side-by-side buildings of logs, slabs, false fronts, and more. Only one building showed itself to be of stone and standing two stories with a sign across the front that showed itself to be the biggest and only hotel in the town. Others had signs telling of the businesses from mercantile to hardware to miner's supplies and more. One boldly proclaimed itself to be a meat market and another as a gunsmith. At the end of the road, the Nevada Livery and Blacksmith stood tall with a corral attached and holding several horses and mules.

Although both hillsides showed prospect holes and dumps, none appeared to be working mines, but further up the valley, both sides of the little creek held claims with wall tents or cabins, sluice boxes and rocker boxes, and more. Butted up against the north facing slope were several stamp mills, smoke stacks showing black smoke as the bigger buildings chugged away with the noisy stamping process.

They rode through town, and even at this early hour, the businesses were showing activity with wagons, horses, and more at the hitchrail and boardwalks busy with men. Cord had been told this was the working man's town and many of the miners that worked some of the bigger mines in Central City and Black Hawk, lived and sometimes worked here. It was not unusual for prospectors to work their own claims, and go down to other mines and work for several days for pocket money. Most of the men in Nevada City were either Cornish or Irish, men that were used to hard labor and willing to do the dirty work.

The passing of two riders that did not have the typical look of prospectors caught a little attention, but nothing more than lingering if not friendly, looks. At the north end of the businesses, Cord spotted a café that had a sign Bowgie Fayre, and nudged Kwitcher to the hitchrail. He nodded to Tabby, "We'll have us some breakfast, listen to the talk."

They pushed through the door, saw several people already seated at both the long counter and the several tables, but there were a couple open tables, so Cord led the way to one near the window. They were seated, doffed their hats and heard a few responses to seeing the long brown hair of Tabby fall over her shoulders. Without the hat and the collar of the duster, her beauty showed and Cord noticed several of the men craning to see her. An aproned man came to their table, asked, "Vedo whye cawas tabm?"

Cord frowned, glanced around and said, "Uh, we'd like some breakfast, if that's what you asked. Do you have any specials?"

"Ess, we haf' fresh eggs and bacon with biscuits and gravy."

Cord glanced to Tabby who nodded, and he turned back to the aproned man, "That will be fine for both of us."

The man nodded and turned away, hurrying to the kitchen.

Cord glanced around the café, saw several frowns of working men that were surprised to see a woman, but also strangers that were not miners. When Cord looked at them, they turned back to their own table or group and continued with their eating. Several were talking but many were speaking in the Cornish

brogue and some in an Irish brogue that neither Cord
not Tabby could discern very well. But when a group
at a nearby table spoke, their talk was easily understood for they were upset about a recent fight with
some men that tried to steal their pokes.

When the waiter brought their food, Cord
noticed the conversation about the outlaws was
spreading around the tables as men leaned toward
others and shared what they heard. By the time Cord
and Tabby were finishing their meal, one of the men
near the counter stood and lifted his hands for the
attention of others. As they quieted and looked to the
man, he began to share what had been discussed. He
spoke in English, although it was with a Cornish
accent, but easily understood. "Men, we have to be
on the watch for those men that hit Paddy's claim.
He took a couple bullets but he's going to make it,
but they took his stash of gold 'fore they run off.
From what Davies said, there were four or five of
them, led by a big man who done the shootin'."

"But what can we do? We've got to work our
claims just to make 'nuff to live!"

"Yeah, but we need to watch out for others,
maybe work together?" asked the speaker, receiving
nods and murmurs from the listeners. The talk
continued but nothing was settled. It was then that
Cord rose, lifted his hand, and when the man that
had started the talking nodded, and said, "You're
new, you have something?"

Cord nodded, looking about, "We've been after

these men for a while now. They hit several claims near Black Hawk, and before that over to Oro City and other places. The leaders are former Jayhawkers or Bushwhackers, but not all were a part of that. Some are new recruits and their numbers change, but they're dangerous and have no qualms about killing anybody. If there is any way you can work together, maybe four or five or more to a claim, that's about the only way to defend yourselves. They will overcome any less."

One of the men at the tables spoke up, "Why are you hunting them?"

"I'm a federal marshal and I've been chasin' after 'em for some time now."

"If you're a marshal, why ain't you got 'em 'fore now?"

"When I started, there were fifteen of them, now not so many." He left unsaid about the number of bodies that have been left on the trail both by Cord and by the outlaws. Cord glanced to Tabby who was staring at him with disbelief and a deep frown, but she said nothing.

"Are you going to be around our claims?" asked another.

"I'll be around, but I make it a point of not being seen. These men do not know I'm a federal marshal, and there's only one or two that have ever seen me and lived. But," he glanced to Tabby and back to the men, "I will be around as much as possible." Cord sat down, and as he reached for his coffee, Tabby whispered, "You're a marshal?"

Cord grinned, nodded, and said, "Yup."

When they left the café, Cord said, "Let's go upstream, maybe look at some of the claims, maybe find us a camp in the trees, *if* we can find any trees!" He shook his head as he stepped aboard Kwitcher, and with a glance to Tabby, reined around and started up the street, but calling it a street was more of an exaggeration as it sloped from the north to the south, with the businesses on the south side of the street a good three feet lower than those on the north.

As they rode west, following the wagon road that sided the little creek, they passed several working claims, men watching them suspiciously as they rode past, but with Tabby's long hair showing and since she traded her duster for her shorter rough-out chore coat, it was obvious she was a woman and men looked after her as she passed. Cord chuckled at how easily men's attention is garnered as most of the prospectors stopped their rocker boxes, or stopped shoveling into the sluice boxes, to watch as they kept to the wagon road.

Tabby just smiled and said, "Why didn't you say something about being a marshal?"

"Why?"

"Well, cuz, I would have liked to know that."

"I just prefer that most don't know. It changes the way people act and such."

"You don't wear a badge either," stated a frowning Tabby.

"Same reason. If folks see the badge, they spread the word, and the outlaws either hide out or use it as a target."

"Hmmm, never thought o' that," mumbled Tabby.

24

VIGILANTES

"I'm tellin' ya, it's the same woman! The one we grabbed and were gonna use her to get the claim an' such down there by Black Hawk, but we got hit an' Jim Bob and Henry got kilt! Yeah, that's the one!" declared Bill Coogan, standing on the opposite side of the table where the others were seated. He was talking to Newt Morrison but looked at the others as well. The group was dumbstruck, shaking their heads, and looking at one another.

Morrison growled, "Can't be! We left her behind at that claim, she's gotta be dead, just like the two at the claim!"

"What about the one that was shootin' from the trees, the one that kilt those two new men?"

"I think that was the same one that was back to Tincup, had that injun woman with him."

"You said he was dead!" snarled James Flood,

shaking his head and grabbing the whiskey bottle to pour himself another shot.

"Thought he was! I shot him! Saw him fall, saw the blood! He wasn't movin', but..." he shrugged as he shook his head.

"Wal, she was with a lanky lookin' fella, had on a duster and hat, whiskers, looked like somebody you'd want to walk around and keep shy of, least-ways that's what I thought," stammered Buck. "An' I tol that new man, Milo Slater, to follow 'em, find their camp."

"Where'd you see 'em?" growled Newt.

"Ridin' west up the draw, had a pack mule with 'em."

"Then here's what we're gonna do," began Newt, scooting his chair closer to the table and motioning the others near. Even Bill Coogan pulled out a chair and sat down, intent on what Morrison was planning.

———

NEVADA CITY WAS a community of the working man, mostly Cornish and Irish imports, men that were tired of the coal mines of their homelands. Men that had come to America when they heard of the fortunes to be had in gold country. Some had come to the San Francisco area with the gold rush of '49, others had come later with the gold rush of the Rockies in '59. One of those that had been in San

Francisco was Cadan Bligh, and it was he who had passed word to the others of an emergency meeting in the church. When the men had gathered, he stood before them, hands uplifted for their attention and silence, and began, "Men, as most of you know, some of our brothers have been killed by claim jumpers, thieves and murderers they are, and we can expect help from no one other than ourselves!" he declared, looking around at the gathered men, many appearing as having climbed from the pits, shafts, or diggings hereabouts. They looked at one another, mumbling and nodding, but listening to Cadan.

An Irishman, Conor Byrnes, stood and asked, "Aye, an' din't we hear 'bout a marshal wha' come into our town?"

"That you did. But he talked a little in the eatery, said he had been chasin' 'em, but we din't see nor hear of any plans he had to do more than chase 'em. That's why we're here, we can't count on him." He paused, looking at the men as many nodded their heads, some elbowing others and agreeing. Cadan continued, "When I was in San Francisco, there was a gang of men, bad'ns they was, called the Sydney Ducks Gang, they'd killed many of the miners an' more, but we formed a Committee of Vigilance, took care of 'em, we did. Sent 'em back to Australia!" He nodded as he spoke, grinning as the others cheered and laughed.

One of the men in the front row, among a group of Cornish miners, stood, "I'm Gerren Tremayne, an'

I've got a good claim, I'm seein' more an' more color, an' I ain't about to give it up to anyone. I've got a double-barreled shotgun loaded with shot, glass, salt, an' rocks and I'll pepper the britches of any man that comes near!"

"And what're you gonna do when they come after you, five or six of 'em, from all sides. That shotgun only has two barrels and they'd take you an' all your dust an' your diggin's too!" called an Irishman, Kayle Bohannan, from behind him.

"Aye, Aye," called several, others with, "Hear, hear!"

Declan Callaghan, an Irishman who stood along the wall, asked, "How we goin' to do it?"

Cadan answered, "We have enough men to make four, five, groups. Each group having six men. Each group with a leader and we patrol the claims, but those that are not patrolling will work together at each claim so no man is by himself. Outlaws like to pick on weaknesses, and any claim with one or two would be weak, but with five or six, we can defend it."

"But that would leave some claims without any defenders!" asked another Irish man, Aiden Ahern.

"That's why we have the patrols, and the working groups will always be near enough to any unattended claims to respond," answered Cadan.

This discussion continued, ideas offered, some accepted, others rejected, but at the end of the meeting, there were six teams, each selecting their own commander. Three Cornish led by Opie Curnow, Lowen Penna, and Gerren Tremayne, each man given the honorary office of Captain. Three Irish teams led by Captains Aiden Ahern, Kayle Bohannan, and Declan Callaghan. Cadan Bligh and Conor Byrnes would serve as co-commanders of the entire brigade, and the patrols were to begin immediately. Many of the men were former soldiers in the civil war, but a few were recent arrivals from over the pond and their only familiarity with firearms was hunting for meat, but their commitment and determination was unwavering. This was their new life, this was their opportunity for dreams to become reality, this was the fulfillment of long-held desires and plans for prosperity and to never work in the coal mines again and to build a life for a family.

————

CORD AND TABBY rode side by side and at each passing of a working claim, he nodded or waved as they passed. He spotted a rider that might be following them, and he told Tabby, "I think that fella back there might be following us. We'll move into the trees there," he gestured to the shoulder of the hillside on the left or south side of the draw, where the creek bent around the point from the flanks of Bald Mountain, "and as soon as we're in the trees, I'm gonna drop off, you take the reins of Kwitcher, and keep goin' while I wait an' see if he follows."

"How far do I go?" questioned Tabby, frowning at Cord.

"Until you find a good campsite or clearing, it won't be far."

He nudged Kwitcher from the trail, Blue at his side, and they climbed the bit of embankment and faded into the trees. Cord dropped to the ground, rifle in hand and he waved to Tabby to keep going. He moved through the trees, his steps silenced by the deep carpet of pine needles, and he moved behind the trunk of a big ponderosa. He waited, watching the trail and the breaks in the trees for any movement, but none came. But still he waited, until his patience wore thin and he started to the edge of the trees for a look into the valley below. Sheltered under a big spruce, he dropped to one knee, searching the draw and the road beside the creek, but nothing moved. He believed the man had turned around or disappeared into the trees himself, but he could see no sign of his passing.

Cord glanced to the sky, saw the gathering dark bottomed clouds and knew there was a storm coming. He turned away from the valley and started after Tabby. She had already made a camp of sorts, the horses and mule had been stripped, gear was stacked under a big spruce with wide spreading branches, and she even had a fire circle with a hat-sized fire going and the coffee pot sitting nearby. She heard him approach, "Anything?" she asked.

"No, maybe I'm just getting jumpy or too cautious."

"Is there any such thing as too cautious?"

Cord chuckled, "Looks like a storm comin', I'll gather some branches, make us a lean-to to keep us dry."

Tabby smiled, "I'm fixin' some sourdough biscuits to go with the venison stew. If you see any tubers or anything that'll go with, fetch it back."

"Fetch it? Sounds like you think I'm some kinda dog," he chuckled.

———

THIS WAS the first time they were so close. With the lean-to providing shelter from the storm, yet with separate bedrolls, it was close quarters. Cord lay awake for some time, he was used to looking at the stars, hands behind his head, and giving thought to prayer and plans for the coming day. Tabby would typically turn in and be asleep within a few minutes, but Cord was a little restless, tossing and turning, and she broke the silence, "Havin' trouble gettin' to sleep, are ya?"

"Yeah. I'm used to lookin' at the stars, maybe doin' a little prayin' an' such." He paused, moved around a little, "And there's a drip back here..."

Tabby smiled in the darkness, "At least you're not snoring as usual. First time I heard that I thought a bear was comin' into camp!" she giggled.

"I do not snore!" declared an indignant Cord, flopping about, kicking at the covers and more.

"How do you know you don't snore?" asked Tabby, smiling in the darkness and laughing to herself.

"I stayed awake one night and listened, never snored a lick!" declared Cord, sounding serious.

"Try it again, and maybe I can get some sleep," suggested Tabby.

———

THE RAIN HAD LET UP, a slight breeze whispered through the trees, and the sky was showing spots of grey among the dark clouds when Cord came awake. He guessed it to be between five and six, and he glanced to Tabby who was sound asleep yet with a smile on her face. Cord smiled, and quietly and slowly slipped from his blankets, pulled on his boots, and with rifle in hand, slipped from the lean-to to greet the day.

25

ASSAULT

The sun was just beginning to show color in the eastern sky when Cord climbed from the lean-to. He stuffed his Bible in his belt, hung the binoculars from his shoulder, took the Winchester in hand and started his climb to the crest of the bluff where he would spend his time with the Lord and watch the rising of the sun. He moved quietly through the timber, the carpet of pine needles still wet and his movements were measured. His thoughts were on Tabby and his future, thinking about his long quest for vengeance or justice, while the pale morning light filtered through the pines. His contemplation did little to help him focus on the faint game trail that was taking him ever higher.

He saw the stab of flame from the darkness of shadows, felt the hard impact to the side of his head and heard the blast of the rifle as the sound echoed across the valley. The sudden excruciating pain knocked him sideways, another sudden, piercing, driving pain hit him in the back, spinning him around only to catch another shock just to the side of his belt buckle. The last jolt bent him over and he crashed into the pine needles face first just as the blanket of darkness slowly enveloped him in silence. He gasped for breath, had a sudden frightening thought of Tabby, and consciousness slipped silently away.

————

TABBY HEARD the racketing of rifle fire and it brought her upright, grabbing for her rifle, as the lean-to crashed in around her and shouts of men frightened her. She fought against the crashing, tried to scramble free of the pine boughs that had made the lean-to, but hands grabbed at her and jerked her to her feet, one man behind her, another in front, both with neckerchiefs covering their faces. One growled, "You're comin' with us, missy!" and she was jerked forward as the same man barked orders to another, "Get ever'thin'! Gear, horses, everthin'!"

Tabby struggled, trying to free her arms from the grip of the man, but the more she struggled, the tighter the grip and searing pain lanced through her arms, making her stop. "Let me go!" she screamed, but the masked man turned and viciously slapped her face, twisting her head and sending a burning pain across her face and neck. She went limp, head drooping, light fading, and darkness covered her mercifully.

———

"CADAN, you 'member that woman what was with that fella said he was a marshal?" asked Gerren Tremayne as the two men stood near the cabin of Cadan.

"Yeah, why?"

"You 'member that flashy horse she was ridin'?"

"Yeah," responded Cadan, turning to face his friend, but frowning at the man. He was known for taking the long way around to get anything said and Cadan was not a patient man.

"I saw that horse, and maybe the one that the marshal rode, ain't sure 'bout his though."

"Where'd you see the horse?"

"There was a bunch o' fellas ridin' up at the west end of the draw, you know, up past the claim of McDougal. An' they had that horse, but nobody was ridin' it. I looked as close as I could, but I ain't sure."

"You're not sure about what? The horse?"

"No, I ain't sure if'n they had the woman or not. She mighta' been with 'em, cuz one was ridin' double. That's what caught my eye, why was they ridin' double when there were two extra horses?"

"Did you see the marshal?"

"No, no, none of 'em looked like the marshal, an' the one what was ridin' double, the big man was behind the saddle an' a littler one was in the saddle," surmised Gerran, looking thoughtful as he tried to remember the details.

"And when did you see them?" asked Cadan.

"Oh, it was this mornin' early, I was just comin' from my outhouse an' they come from the trees, movin' quick, but I don' know why they was goin' up the road, it don't go much further, you know. Only thing up there was that ol' claim of ol' Wynkoop an' he abandoned that couple year ago. 'Course he did have a cabin up there in the trees..." he mumbled the last, turning to go down to the diggings.

Cadan called him back, "Did you hear that gunfire early this mornin', just 'fore the sun came up. Sounded like it came from up in the trees, or maybe even up by Wynkoop's claim."

"Yeah, I heared it, thought somebody was huntin' and weren't a good 'nuff shot. They was only a few shots, maybe three or four, weren't much," drawled Gerren.

Cadan glanced at the sun, guessed it to be goin' on mid-morning and looked at Gerren, "You seen Declan and the vigilantes?"

"No, they ain't been up this far yet. Was they comin' thisaway?"

"Should be showin' up real soon. I'll put more coffee on..." said Cadan, his frustration with the slow talking and slow thinking of Gerran Tremayne showing as he turned into his cabin.

THE ROCKING of the horse's gait brought Tabitha back to consciousness. She sat still, feeling the man behind her, and looked around but saw only a trace of a trail and thick trees, pines and firs and more. Her captor grunted with the rocking gait, and Tabby felt the bulge under her rough-out chore coat. She had removed her pistol from the holster and put it in the inside pocket of her coat, it was a practice she had established when they first came to gold country. The holster would not always be near, but she used her coat as an extra cover while she slept. When she first heard the gunshots, she sat up and put on her coat, listening, but the next thing that happened was when the lean-to crashed down around her and hands grabbed at her to pull her to her feet. With first light, she recognized the rider before them, but could not turn to see the man that held her in his saddle.

They reined up beside an older log cabin and a quick glance told her it was a miner's cabin that sat near the ore dump of his mine, but neither had been used for some time. The man behind her slid to the ground and reached up for her. It was her first look at the man and she was repulsed and pulled back from his reach, "You!" she exclaimed, trying to pull away from his reach.

The big man grabbed her arm and growled, "Git down here!"

"You're the same one!" she shouted, looking around and recognizing two of the others, "All of you! You killed my brothers!" she shouted again, anger biting every word. But she was soon silenced when Newt Morrison dragged her off the horse and pulled her against him, his meaty paw covering her mouth.

"Shut up! Not another word!" he barked, wrapping his arms around her and lifting her off the ground, her feet kicking at the air as she twisted and squirmed. Morrison just pulled her tight and cackled, "Tha's alright, just keep it up, I'll just hafta squeeze it outta ya'!"

Morrison tucked her under one arm like a bag of potatoes and grabbed the door handle, jerking it open as he stepped in the door. Tabby was still squirming and kicking and he slapped her on the rear, open-handed, cackling, "Just keep it up, missy, keep it up. I can do this all day. I don't mind," and paddled her again, laughing. He walked across the crowded room, dumped her on a cot, and sat down on the edge, his back to her.

The others crowded into the cabin and Buck Smithers asked, "When do we get a turn? Hehehe-he..." as he stepped to the side to see the woman behind Morrison.

"Ain't no turns, she's mine! Got it! Mine!"

"Whatchu gonna do with her, Newt," asked Coogan, grabbing a chair and sitting at the table.

"Dunno yet, gotta think 'bout it!"

"I got some idee what to do," cackled James Flood, joining Coogan at the table.

Newt glared at both men at the table, "You two get a fire goin' and fix us some breakfast!"

"Yeah, that's a good idea, but what about her? Can she cook?" asked the newest of the bunch, Milo Slater.

"She ain't doin' nuthin'!" snarled Morrison, and ordered, "You go get the pannier with the food and help 'em fix breakfast!"

A grumbling Milo dropped his eyes and trudged to the door, glancing to the cot and Newt and the woman, then pushed open the door and stepped into the bright light from the rising sun that stood just above the treetops. Morrison moved to the table and began sharing his plans for the day. "We're gonna take those two claims at the head of the draw! Both of 'em just have one man and it'll be easy, and dependin' on how much we get, we might just leave this part of the country and head southwest, maybe try Breckenridge. This place is gettin' too crowded!"

The others were fidgeting with the breakfast makings but Coogan looked at Morrison, "How much is enough?"

"Couple good pouches full of dust'd do it. That'd be enough to keep us outfitted till we get to Breckenridge."

"What about her?" asked Flood, nodding toward Tabitha who had retreated to the shadows at the edge of the bunk against the wall.

"We'll leave her here, maybe with one man. Then come back after her when we finish with those two claims." He leaned forward at the table, started drawing in the dust, "See, we're here, just below the point of the hill behind us. The trail to Nevada City goes along the crick, like this," drawing in the dust with a squiggly line, "and we can go over that ridge and drop into York Gulch and on south to Clear Creek Canyon. That'll take us west an' south to Georgetown, and on to Breckenridge. Might even hit some claims around Georgetown."

Flood and Coogan looked at each other and back to Morrison, slowly nodding their heads and Flood pointed to the dust map, "An' if anybody's lookin' for us, they'll think we headed down the crick to town or past that and further on..." he cackled, "but we'll be goin' over the hill! I like it, ummhmm." He grinned as he worked the dough for the biscuits and placed them in the Dutch oven.

26

CONFUSION

IT WAS NOTHING MORE THAN A SPRING-FED CREEK THAT fell from the upper reaches of Bald Mountain and cascaded through the gulch to make its way to Nevada City, and it was near the headwaters of this creek that Cadan Bligh and Gerran Tremayne had their claims, the last two claims on this creek. Declan Callaghan led the band of six vigilantes as they made their first patrol of the gulch and it was nearing midday when they approached Cadan's claim where the two men were working the sluice, one shoveling ore into the sluice, the other adjusting the upper end of the sluice and the flow of the water. Declan hailed the pair, "Dia duit!"

Cadan waved, "Dydh da'!" and dropped the shovel, motioned to Gerran to stop the water, and they watched as Declan and the group crossed the creek to join them. "So, everything go alright?"

"Aye, aye. No trouble, no sign of trouble,"

answered Declan, motioning to the others to get down.

"We've got coffee on, put the horses around back behind the cabin, then come in the back door."

"Aye, we'll be doin' that alright," he responded, motioning to the men what to do.

Cadan had gone into the cabin and the others were putting their horses in the corral when Gerran came running in, "Riders comin'! Looks like five or more, an' they ain't miners!"

The men glanced to one another, Cadan grabbed his rifle from the rack near the bunks and Gerran grabbed his that was standing by the door. The other men scrambled out the back door, getting their weapons from their saddles.

Cadan stepped out the door, his rifle at his side and started to the sluice. The riders splashed across the creek, pistols and rifles in hand and the leader growled, "Drop that rifle!" lifting his own rifle to threaten Cadan. But Cadan was not to be bluffed or threatened and dove behind a big rock that had been left near the sluice just as the rifle roared and a bullet whanged off the rock. It was that first shot that opened the fight, and the raiders were surprised when rifles roared from both sides of the cabin and two from the door and window that faced the draw.

The leader of the raiders flinched, and fell forward onto the pommel of his saddle as he jerked the head of his horse around, digging his heels into the ribs of the animal and splashing into the little creek. Bullets were flying and another of the raiders was struck, the multiple bullets driving him out of the saddle to fall face down in the creek. The others had already turned to flee, but another man took a bullet, fell forward on the neck of his horse but held on to make it to the trees on the far side of the road, following the leader, Newt Morrison. Two others scattered, one up the trail, the other downstream, both lying low on the necks of their animals as the horses kicked up dirt to make their getaway.

The shooting stopped as quickly as it started and the vigilantes came from behind the cabin as Cadan rose from behind the rock and Gerran came from the door. They looked at one another, fearful eyes showing white, and breath coming in gasps, but as they looked at each other and saw no blood, they relaxed and grins replaced frowns and they came close, slapping shoulders and backs, laughing and talking, shaking their heads and cheerfully commenting on their success. "We done it boys! We done it!" declared Cadan, looking around the group, slowly letting themselves relax.

It had been a quick victory for the working men of the vigilantes of Nevada City. The only dead man one of the raiders that still lay in the creek below the sluice box, but the vigilantes would continue their patrols for the rest of the summer with no other confrontations. There was no way for them to know that this was the only gang of outlaws that dared to attempt their thievery in this part of gold country, and once confronted, it was easy for them to leave in search of easier pickings.

————

Milo Slater had been left at the cabin with Tabitha Townsend. He was a man that had respect for women, but he also feared Newt Morrison, and was not about to allow Tabitha any extra freedom, knowing he would have to answer to the others for any mishap. When the others left the cabin, Tabby slowly came from the shadows to sit on the edge of the bunk and look around. "Are you the only one left?"

"That's right, but don't try anything. I don't wanna hafta shoot a woman!" declared a determined Milo, scowling at Tabby.

"Uh, what's your name?"

"Milo, Milo Slater. Why?"

"I want to know what to call you, Milo. Uh, I need to, uh, you know, go?" asked Tabby, giving a pleading look to the lone man.

"But, I can't let you do that, not till the others get back!"

"Oh, come on. I have to, baadd," she pleaded, putting her hands on her lower tummy as if to hold herself from an accident.

"I can't, if they come back an..."

"I promise I won't do anything. They'll never know, pleeeease?"

He looked around, shaking his head, pulled his pistol from the holster, cocked the hammer and said, "Alright, you go first," pointing to the door.

"Oh, thank you, thank you," responded Tabby, rising and bent over, she waddled to the door, trying to show embarrassment.

Milo followed close behind, and once outside, he said, "Outhouse is aroun' back," he motioned with the pistol. Tabby moved as directed, spotted the outhouse and stepped inside. Once out of sight, she sat down, felt for the pistol in the inside pocket of her jacket and smiled at the comforting feel of the Colt Baby Dragoon Pocket revolver. She knew it was loaded and she was ready to use it. She stood, pushed open the door and stepped out. She had spotted her horse in the corral, tethered to the top rail and saw the saddle on the fence rail, but Cord's grulla and the mule were gone. She saw the top and second rail of the fence broken down and thought, *They musta broke an' run, but my Cassi was tied, thank goodness.* She looked at Milo. He had holstered his pistol, and smiled as she came out and motioned for her to go before him back to the front of the cabin. She took a couple steps, frowned, and leaned to the side as if to look around the corner of the cabin, saw Milo frown and turn to look where she looked, and she pulled the pistol from the pocket and held it before her when he turned back to face her.

His eyes flared and he stepped back, lifted his

hand as if to stop any bullet and stuttered, "Wh, wh, where'd you get that?"

"It was in my pocket all the time," softly answered a smiling Tabby. She waved the pistol, "Now catch up my horse and saddle it!"

"But you can't do that, Newt'll kill me!" pleaded the man.

"If you don't, I'll hafta shoot you first!" answered a smiling Tabby.

"Ah, you won't shoot me, you're a woman!"

"Yes, I'm a woman, but why can't I shoot you?"

"Well, cuz..." began Milo, taking a step closer and extending his hand as if he expected her to hand over the pistol.

"Don't!" ordered Tabby, "I don't want to shoot you, cuz then I'll hafta saddle my own horse, but I will..." she declared, bringing the pistol to full cock. The racketing sound of the cocking hammer seemed to fill the void of the trees as she motioned with the pistol for him to go to the corral.

"I can't, I just can't..." he pleaded, starting to step closer.

Tabby knew he was trying to get within reach of her pistol to grab it away from her, but she held her ground. "Milo, look where I'm pointing this pistol, and notice, it's not at your head, but lower. You see Milo, I don't want to kill you, but that belt buckle makes a good target, now if I..." she carefully lowered the muzzle of the pistol, and looked down the barrel.

Milo watched her, saw the barrel lower, and

unconsciously put both hands below his buckle, until she said, "A little lower, Milo..." and grinned.

"You wouldn't do that...please, no..."

"Then saddle my horse!"

"I can't," he pleaded, extending his hands to implore her.

She shook her head and pulled the trigger, the pocket pistol bucked and roared, flame spat from the barrel and the .36 caliber slug drove itself into the upper thigh of Milo, dropping him to his knees and down on his back.

He screamed, grabbing at himself, and rolled to look at his leg, looked up at her, "You shot me! You really shot me!"

"I said I would, Milo. Now, you just lay there while I saddle my horse, and don't move now, cuz next shot will be a little closer, you know."

She rode from the cabin, leaving Milo where he lay but only after she brought him some rags to put on his wound. She did not know if he would bleed out and die or not, but at this point, she felt a bitter satisfaction knowing she had exacted at least some vengeance on those that had killed her brothers. But now, she had to find Cord. Although she had heard the two men tell their leader, the big man called Newt, about how they shot Cord at least three times, saw him go down, and saw his body bleeding and bloody head, "That bullet to his head killed him, he was bleedin' like a stuck hog! I know he was dead."

She just could not accept that, she had already

lost her brothers, and could not lose the only friend she had left, he *had* to be alive, and if he was still alive and needed nursing, she could and would do it, whatever was necessary. But first, she had to find him. She had heard the rattle of gunfire from below, apparently coming from the bottom of the draw, probably the gang hitting one of the claims, *I need to cut through the trees, can't be found by them!* As her sorrel mare, Cassi, picked her way through the trees, she remembered she had seen Cord's horse, Kwitcher, when she was taken from the camp, but he was not in the corral.

She thought about what they might need, probably some bandages and medicine for Cord, but they had taken the panniers and more. But did they? She did not remember seeing them with anything but her horse and saddle, and the grulla stallion of Cord's. She had put the parfleche of food in the lean-to to keep it from the rain, and they had not taken it, nor the bedrolls...she thought, frowning, trying to remember just what had been taken. Cord had covered the packs, panniers, and more with branches much like the lean-to, knowing the branches would shed water and help keep them from the worst of the weather, but...she pondered the thought, mindlessly letting her big sorrel, Cassi, find her way.

———

It was a cold nose and a wet tongue that brought Cord awake. He opened his eyes to see the face of Blue, grinning and trying to lick his face. Cord put his hand out, touched behind the dog's ears, but the pain made him lift his hand and touch his head, thinking he had been hit with a sledge hammer. Then his memory began to return, he slowly sat up, leaned against the rough bark of the nearest ponderosa, saw the dried pool of blood, shook his head and looked at his hand that came away from his head with fresh blood. He looked down at his chest, blood covered his shirt and he felt under the shirt. He found what was the exit wound from a bullet, it tore through his back and exited his side, low down, just above his belt. He winced as he tried to move and tried to breathe deep, but pain seared through his midriff, making him grab at his belt. His Bible was torn and he pulled it from his belt to see the hole through the front leather, but not out the back. The Bible had taken the bullet, but the impact had bruised his stomach muscles and might have broken a lower rib. He winced again as he tried to move; he was weak, but knew he had to move and find something to stop the bleeding. He tried to get up, but his head dropped to his chest and he lost consciousness again.

27

RESOLUTION

THE MARE STOPPED, HEAD HIGH, EARS PRICKED AND nostrils flaring as she snorted, grew tense and side-stepped. Tabby leaned forward, staring into the timber but saw nothing. She reached down and stroked the mare's neck, "Easy girl. What is it? What do you see?" and nudged the sorrel forward. She picked her way carefully through the trees until the little clearing that had been their camp showed. Tabby reined up, stood in her stirrups, looking around, and was surprised to see Cord's grulla stallion standing tall and looking at the mare and the mule, just past him in the trees, but looking over Kwitcher's back at her. A smile broke her face as Tabby nudged her mount forward, chuckling at what the outlaws would think when she and the animals were gone. She was not surprised to see the big stallion and mule, knowing they would return to their last camp, looking for Cord.

She looked around, saw the trampled ruins of the lean-to, and stepped down to retrieve the parfleche with the food. She stood looking around and saw the pile of limbs that hid the panniers and more under the big spruce with long limbs stretching wide to cover the gear. The stallion had come near, sniffing around the mare, low rumbles coming from both animals. Tabby stepped close to Kwitcher, "Where is he? Where's Cord, Kwitcher?" but the stallion was only interested in the sorrel mare.

Tabby frowned, *What about Blue? Where's the dog?* She thought about the ever present and faithful dog, knowing that if possible, he would be with Cord. She looked at the trees, saw the faint trail that split the trees, and quickly started up the trail. She had gone no more than thirty or forty yards when she spotted the dog and Cord leaning against a tree, but he was not moving.

Tabby went to his side and dropped to the ground beside him, reaching out to touch his head where the bullet had plowed a furrow through his hair and showed matted hair and clotted blood. She frowned, looking him over, saw the bloody shirt and side, pulled open the shirt to reveal the bloody wound, blood still seeping from the clotted mass. She looked around, rose and with a glance back to Cord said, "I'll be right back, don't move!" and trotted back to the camp. She tossed aside the branches, digging for the pannier that had the parfleche with the medical supplies. She grabbed it up and ran back to Cord's side. She dropped back down to his side and withdrew several pieces of cloth that could be made into a pad for the wounds. She dug in the parfleche, remembering Cord telling her about an ointment made from the buds of the aspen called Balm of Gilead. She found the tin with the ointment, and another that he said was Osha or Bear Root. She thought, *if one is good, two is better!* and after cleaning the wounds on his side, back, and head, she made cloth pads covered with the ointments and applied them, used long strips of cloth to hold them in place, and sat back, looking at the unconscious man, shaking her head.

She took a deep breath and poured water on another piece of cloth and began washing his face and neck, all the while trying to figure out how she could get him back to camp, and smiled as she thought, *why not move camp up here?* Looking around, she saw where she could make a fire ring, there were big trees for shelter and a place to picket the animals. She nodded to herself, stood and trotted back to camp to bring the animals and their gear back to their new campsite.

She stretched out Cord's bedroll, picked the pine needles and such from the remains of the caved-in lean-to, and lay it next to where Cord was leaning against the tree. She looked at Blue, "Sure wish you could help me!" she declared and began working to get him down on the blankets. Once down, she checked his bandages, added more bandaging, and satisfied, turned away and started the fire ring. She knew he would be wanting some coffee, if and when he came awake.

She kept herself busy setting up camp, starting the cookfire, getting the coffee going, and more. With the gear stacked and stashed under cover of pine boughs, the animals on a picket line, bedrolls arranged, and the pannier with the foodstuffs nearby, she was satisfied with her work. Then she looked at the animals, realized it had been a while since they had water and graze and decided to take them down to the creek on the north side of the butte, away from the many claims. It would be just a short jaunt and they needed the water, but she hated to leave Cord.

———

CORD CAME AWAKE, his eyes slitted as he looked around without moving, and frowned when he saw the gear stacked nearby, the fire ring with the coffeepot, and some tin cups on the rock beside it, and a picket line stretched between two trees, but no animals. He forced himself to sit up, felt the stabbing pain of his wounds and winced, his hand going to his head, felt the bandage and felt at his side and then yet another bandage. *Who? When?* And where was Tabby? Was she taken, and—his questions were answered when he heard the clatter of horses coming from the trees on the far side of the bluff and

Tabby showed herself, leading the animals, and with a broad smile showing as she looked at Cord.

"How long have I been out? And how did you get me here? Were you taken?" he asked, frowning and confused.

"Uh, hold on a minute, I'll answer all your questions, but, let me check your wounds." She picketed the animals and went to his side, knelt beside him and checked his bandages, "You're still bleeding some from this one," she said, looking at his side, and tenderly touching the area around the wound. "I'll need to change that bandage soon, but first, let's get some food in you!"

Tabby had propped him up with one of the panniers and an extra blanket, brought him some strip steaks that had been broiled over the open fire, a couple of Indian potatoes she had baked in the coals, and a big cup of steaming black coffee. He was pleased with the food, struggled to get it all down, but soon lay back and dropped off to sleep. Tabby covered him with the blankets, did her best to make him comfortable, fed herself, and did a walk around, rifle in hand, to try to ensure their isolation and safety.

It was a clear sky and the wind had stilled when Tabby returned to camp. She checked on Cord, checked the animals, and made certain all the weapons were loaded. Cord had his pistol in the holster and his Winchester nearby, both had been under him when he was shot and were left behind by the outlaws. Even the Spencer and coach gun were still in the packs that had been overlooked by the raiders and since Kwitcher had returned, the outlaws had netted very little from their raid. She stretched out on her blankets, and with a long look at the stars, finally dropped off to sleep.

CORD AWOKE to the smell of bacon frying, and he looked at the back of Tabby as she fidgeted with the frying pan. He saw the Dutch oven in the coals, smiled and said, "Mmmm, you're makin' me hungry!"

Tabby turned, smiling, "Well, good morning sleepyhead. I was beginning to wonder if you were going to sleep all day."

"I thought about it, but my stomach was growlin' at me so loud, I thought a bear was comin' into camp!"

"Nah, but there was one in camp last night! At least I thought so, but he musta been layin' on the other side of you. Made it hard to sleep with all that growlin'!" she laughed. She dished up some bacon, beans and biscuits, and handed the plate to Cord as he was struggling to sit up. He used the tree to lean against and set about making quick work of the food. He looked at Tabby, "Uh, gravy woulda gone good with those biscuits."

"You ate 'em too fast, I'm just now finishin' the

gravy, but we've got more biscuits." She took his plate, loaded it with biscuits and gravy, and handed it back. He grinned and dug in, making short work of the extended breakfast. He took a deep breath, started to lay back, but Tabby said, "Don't do it! I've got to change your bandages first!"

Although he had asked the questions, she had not been forthcoming with the answers, always too busy with bandaging his wounds, or fixing the food. But now as she replaced the bandages with clean ones, he asked again, "So, what happened?"

She looked at him and began, "It was the Jayhawkers. Same ones that killed my brothers," she growled, shaking her head. "After they shot you, they took me, different ones than shot you cuz I heard them tellin' the big one, the one that had me, how they shot you and were sure you were dead. We went to a cabin up the hill a ways, looked to be one that had been a miner's with his claim, but it was long abandoned. After a while, they left me behind with one name o' Milo Slater, and the rest of 'em went down to hit another claim. While they were gone, I tricked Milo into lettin' me go to the outhouse, then I got the drop on him with my pocket pistol, you know I keep it in the pocket of my coat at night. He didn't think I'd shoot him, so he thought he'd get it away from me, but I shot him!" she declared matter-of-factly, grinning.

"Did you kill him?" asked an astounded Cord, frowning at Tabby.

"Not right off, hit him in the thigh and he was bleedin' purty bad, but I give him a bandage 'fore I left and he was still alive then."

"Hold on. You shot him in the thigh? You're a better shot than that! How far were you from him?"

"Oh, 'bout ten feet."

"Wait, you did that a purpose, din't you?" asked Cord, grinning.

"Had to make him fearful..." snickeredTabby.

"That'd do it, yessiree."

28

RECOVERY

"So, should I be worried about them coming after us again?" asked Cord, looking at Abby as she fussed with his bandages.

"Prob'ly not. When I was at that cabin, I heard 'em say they was goin' after a couple claims, but after they left I heard a bunch of shootin', sounded like a war! And they din't come back right away so I got away alright. I think they mighta got into a fight that cost 'em. After we heard them miners talkin' in the café, I think they got together and helped each other. They mighta done some damage to the outlaws," she surmised as she finished up the bandaging.

She sat back, looking at Cord, "You look a little peak'ed. You better get you some rest, get mended up a bit more."

"We shouldn't take for granted those bush-whackers were done in, not the way they always came out of their scrapes. You need to keep a watch.

You give it a go for a few hours, I'll rest up and then relieve you."

"You can't move! You'll tear everthin' open. As it is, I couldn't sew 'em up and they're gonna take a while to heal. You just rest, me'n Blue will stand watch," declared a determined Tabby.

"Look, you're gonna get tired and then fall asleep and it won't do either one of us any good, so, when you get tired, wake me, and I'll just sit up, stay awake and keep watch thataway and you can get some sleep," he explained, frowning at her as if he would broker no argument.

"Alright, alright, when I get tired, I'll wake you so I can get some sleep," she answered, shaking her head and mumbling, *Men, more stubborn than mules!*

"What'd you say?" asked Cord.

"Nuthin', never mind!" Tabby laughed.

She picked up her rifle and headed into the trees. She sat in the dark, away from the fire and letting her eyes become accustomed to the darkness. With the last gasp of dusk, the darkness fell on the mountains and the big moon, now full, hung lazily in the star-studded sky. Tabby was not in the habit of prayer, but she thought of Cord and his times with the Lord and wondered what she was missing. As a child, she had not been raised in a prayerful family, oh, they went to church on occasion, the white clapboard church at the edge of town that most folks went to, but her Pa was not one to talk about God and the Bible. Whenever her mother asked to go to some special happening at the church, he would usually grumble about it, but eventually give in and they would go as a family. Tabby heard him explain once to a neighbor, "Yeah, we go just to keep muh wife happy, keep her from complainin' 'bout things." And Tabby and her brothers had not gone since the Jayhawkers raid, although most other townsfolks that survived made it a habit.

She looked at the stars that seemed to dance in the heavens and wondered out loud, "So, God, are you really out there? If so, maybe you could help Cord. He's hurtin' somethin' fierce and I'm afraid of losin' him. I can't lose him, he's all I got now." She fell silent and stood quiet, thinking about what she had just said, a thought she had not before verbalized, but one that was in the forefront of her mind, *Cord is all I have! Maybe I oughta talk to him about God, just in case.* The cry of a lonesome coyote brought her attention back to the moment and she moved from under the tall ponderosa and went into the aspen, finding a spot near one of the bigger trees, and sat down. Overhead an insomniac squirrel scolded the intruder and threw a twig her direction. She chuckled when a nighthawk seemed to scold the squirrel, but the entertainment kept her awake and that's all that was needed.

She kept in the shadows, moving only when she needed to stir herself to wakefulness and it was after midnight when she finally gave up and went to Cord to nudge him awake. He came full awake instantly, started to sit up, but she put her hand on his chest, "No, stay where you are. I need to get some sleep, so here's a rifle, keep it close and when you need to sleep, nudge me. I won't need much, just a little. It's quiet, nothing but birds and such."

Cord nodded, sat up and scooted to the tree beside him, settled himself against it and pulled the blanket over his legs, lifted his own rifle, and said, "Get some rest. Keep your rifle close and I'll wake you if I need to but rest easy." Tabby nodded, and turned in to her blankets, pulled them up around her shoulder and was soon sound asleep.

———

AFTER CHANGING his bandages the next morning, Tabby looked at Cord, "You're going to have to heal up soon, we're running low on that salve you have."

Cord grinned, "If you take the horses to water, look for some huckleberry, maybe some onions, and some sage. The leaves of all those can be mashed together and will make a balm or salve that will also help."

Tabby frowned, "How do you know this?"

Cord chuckled, "I had a friend, she was a native, a Capote Ute woman, and she taught me a lot about plants an' such. She made that salve," nodding to the tin, "from the buds of the aspen. It's called the Balm of Gilead, and the other was made from Osha or bear root."

"What's it called?"

"Sage."

Tabby shook her head, "Like I said, you need to heal up so I can smack you, you smart aleck!" She laughed as she gathered up the pans and such after their breakfast. "I'll take the horses to water and see if I can find some sage, onion, and huckleberry. Anything else?"

"It's too late to get any sap from the buds of aspen, but you could look for osha."

"What's it look like?"

"In wet soil by the streams. White flat-topped flowers on long stems," he held up his hand, all fingers extended in a bunch to show the shape of the bloom, "and leaves with many serrations and smells like strong celery. Be sure to bring both the leaves and blooms with you, just to be sure."

Tabby nodded, put away the gear and loosed the animals from the picket line and started to the little creek in the bottom, her rifle hanging from a sling on her shoulder. When she reached the stream, the grassy banks pushed back to the trees, offering a good graze for them and she picketed them within reach of the water and the grass and began her search for sage, huckleberry, and osha plants and roots.

When she returned to camp, she had a parfleche full of her gatherings and Cord grinned as he pulled them from the bag. "You did a great job! Thanks! We'll need a big flat rock and a smaller rock, flat on at least one side. We'll crush these and make a balm out of them. They'll be good for the wounds." Tabby was pleased with the praise and quickly found the rocks for their work and they sat about crushing the plants, making the salve.

Cord said, "I was looking at this wound," motioning to his lower side, "and you might need to do some trimming. The loose skin needs to be cut back so the wound can close and heal."

"You want me to cut you?" asked Tabby, showing her incredulity with a frown.

"Ummhmm, that's what it'll take."

"Never had anyone ask me to cut 'em!" snickered Tabby, grinning at Cord.

"Oh, I'll be watching and guiding you. I just can't see there good enough to do it myself, or I would."

"So, if I wasn't here, you'd do it yourself?"

"Ummhmmm, have to, but I couldn't do as good a job as you."

Cord suddenly went sober, held up his hand for quiet and reached for his rifle. He motioned to Tabby to get her rifle and take to the trees, "Somebody's coming up the trail," he whispered. Tabby quickly did as bidden and disappeared into the trees.

A voice called out, "Hello the camp! Can I come in?"

Cord could not see who was hailing them, but answered, "Come in if you're friendly!"

A figure pushed through the trees, following the dim trail, leading his horse. Cord recognized the man as the speaker from the café and motioned with his rifle, "Have a seat. There's coffee in the pot," he said, motioning to the coffee pot and cups on the rock beside the fire.

"Thank you," answered Cadan Bligh. "I wondered if it might be you camped up here. I saw what I thought was a whiff of smoke but it wasn't much, so thought I'd check it out." As he talked, he looked at Cord, noticing he did not stand, and had a bandage on the side of his head. He nodded to Cord, "What happened?"

Cord knew Tabby was near enough to see him and he motioned for her to come back into the camp and he looked at Cadan Bligh, "I think the Jayhawkers hit us, and might have hit some claims afterward. They attacked us just 'fore daylight a couple days ago, shot me three times, took Tabby there," nodding to Tabby as she came from the trees, rifle at the ready, "but she shot the one left with her, heard the others shootin' up a claim o'er yonder, and she came back, found me and been doctorin' me up ever since."

"It was our claim they were shooting up, as you put it. But we had a surprise for them. We had organized a vigilance group, and they hit my claim just as the band of vigilantes happened to stop for coffee. We killed one, wounded two others and them and the other two ran off. Haven't seen or heard from them since. I think they left! But just to be sure, we knew they came from up toward the flanks of Bald

Mountain and we knew of one abandoned claim and cabin up there, so we rode up there the next day, found it empty. They didn't even bury the man out back of the cabin, looked like he'd been shot in the leg and bled to death."

Cord heard Tabby gasp, shake her head, and move away, knowing she was thinking about the man she shot and that he was the one that bled to death.

"You said you wounded two?" asked Cord.

"That's right," answered Cadan.

"Any sign they went to the cabin?"

"Yes, there were bloody bandages, but that's all."

"So, maybe they did leave," mused Cord, reaching for the coffeepot. He poured himself a cup, poured one for Tabby and refilled Cadan's. He looked pensive for a moment until Tabby said, "I heard them say they might go to Breckenridge and maybe Georgetown after this."

29

CHOICES

THE HORSE THUNDERED UP THE ROAD, THE RIDER shouting, "They's comin', they's comin'!" as he slid his horse to a stop. He twisted in his saddle, pointing down the road that bent through the trees, "I passed that claim we hit, goin' thru the trees I was, an' saw 'em mountin' up. Heard one of 'em say, 'they gotta be in the cabin up the end of the road!' an' he was pointin' thisaway! I din't know if'n you was here or not, but..." he stammered as he looked at the three men that had come from the cabin.

Newt Morrison, James Flood, and Bill Coogan had just gathered at the cabin and now stood in front of the open door. Newt growled, "How many are they?"

"Looked to be at least six, mebbe eight! We gotta hurry, they'll be here right quick!" shouted Buck Smithers, still atop his mount.

Newt said, "Grab your gear an' horses, let's get

into them trees. If they come after us, we can hit 'em from cover!" he ran around the cabin, snatched the reins of his horse that had been standing since he fled from the fight at the claim. He had a bloody bandage at the top of his shoulder at his neck, but he gritted his teeth and tugged on the reins, going to the trees beside the mine shaft. He was followed by the others doing the same. James Flood's jacket was bloody at his middle, and he winced and struggled to lead his horse and make it to the trees. Newt shouted, "Coogan, you follow, try to wipe out our trail, you know, use a branch, scatter some dirt, anything!"

Coogan nodded, handed the lead of his horse to Buck Smithers, and grabbed a branch from a nearby tree and followed the others, sweeping the tracks as best he could. He knew it would not fool a good tracker, but these were miners and the only thing they saw was rocks and such. He heard the clatter of hooves, made a last sweep, and took to the trees. The men had their rifles on the saddles, their pistols in their holsters, and had never bothered to do much in the cabin, although they did have some pots and coffee cups, but nothing of importance. Coogan ducked into the trees, dropped to his knees behind a big spruce, and looked back at the cabin.

Eight men rode up, all holding rifles, and surrounded the cabin, one called out, "Anybody in there, come out with your hands high!"

The men mumbled among themselves, until

Gerran Tremayne told Cadan Bligh, "Nobody's in there, Cadan. Whaddaya want us to do?"

"We'll cover you, go on in the cabin, make sure there's no one there."

Gerran slipped off his mount, held his rifle before him, and banged on the door, "Come outta there you scum!" and stepped back, his rifle at the ready. But nothing happened and with a glance to Cadan, Gerran kicked open the door, looked inside then cautiously walked into the cabin. He could be heard kicking things around, then he came to the door. "Nothin' 'n no one here!"

The voice of Declan Callaghan came from the rear of the cabin, "Aye an' there's a stiff back here, there be, sure 'nuff!"

The others nudged their mounts to the back of the cabin where Declan was standing beside the body of Milo Slater, the bloody bandage at his crotch, his eyes staring at the treetops. "Looks like he's been dead awhile. Don' think he was wit' the others," surmised Declan, glancing from the corpse to Cadan.

Bligh nodded, "Don' know where they went, but I'm hopin' they had enough sense to leave this country. After that run-in down to the claim, if you," looking around at the rest of the men, "are any sample, I'm thinkin' our vigilantes are a little blood-thirsty. I saw it in San Francisco, and once it starts, it won't stop until they're all dead or gone!"

"Aye, an' that's good, is it not?" answered Declan,

to the nods and mumbles of agreement from the others.

"That's what we're all about, sure'n it is!" answered Cadan, reining his horse around to leave. Declan called after him, "Whaddawe do 'bout this'n?" pointing to the corpse.

"The buzzards gotta eat too, but it might make 'em sick. Leave him!"

————

As the vigilantes took the road back toward Nevada City, Flood looked at Morrison, and asked, "You hear what he said about vigilantes?"

"Yeah, that's why they was ready for us at that claim. I ain't run up against vigilantes, but I ain't heard nuthin' good about 'em."

"I was in San Francisco when the vigilantes were organized, started to join 'em, but changed my mind. Good thing too, they hung a half dozen of their own! Vigilantes ain't nuthin' to mess with!" replied Flood as the men rose and filtered from the trees to return to the cabin.

They picketed their horses behind the cabin and Newt told Smithers and Coogan, "You two, do somethin' with that!" pointing to Slater's body. The two men looked at one another, back to Newt, "What?"

"Bury it or drag it off. He'll start stinkin' soon!"

"Already does," mumbled Smithers, motioning Coogan to give him a hand.

Newt and James stepped into the cabin, each sliding a chair to the table and leaned on the table, each man checking his wounds and bandages. Newt grumbled, "What I wanna know, is where's that woman! We left that worthless piece of garbage to guard her and we come back an' he's dead and she's gone! Did somebody come get her?"

"How do I know?" whined Flood, trying to pull his bandage away from his wound. The bullet had driven through his abdomen and out his back, just to the right of his navel, and had done considerable damage on the inside. He was burning up, the pain was excruciating, and he looked at Morrison, "We got any other bandages and such? I'm still bleedin' bad and it hurts like a big horse is standin' on my gut!"

"If those idjits woulda brought the rest of the gear from that fella an' that woman, we'd prob'ly have some, but we ain't got nuthin'!" he growled, putting his hand to his own wound. He had taken a bullet that cut through the muscle atop his shoulder where the neck muscles join. It burned like Hades and he winced with every move. When he had it bandaged, they poured whiskey on the wound, then covered it with folded material and a long strip of material was wrapped over the bandage and under both his arms to hold it secure. But it still showed fresh blood coming through.

"Is there anything that passes for a doctor in Nevada City?" whined Flood.

"No, but there is in Central City." He looked at Flood, then down at his own wound, "But if we try to go down this draw, we'll run into them vigilantes. Mebbe if we wait till dark we can ride through and go to Central City."

"Yeah, yeah, we got some stuff to eat in our packs an' we can get them others to fix it. Then we can rest up till after dark, then we can go. Yeah, we can do that!" declared Flood, pleased with the plan.

———

CORD WAS STILL unable to stand, but he waved as he watched Cadan leave their camp. He glanced to Tabby, "So, whaddaya think?"

"About what?"

"About the bushwhackers that jumped us?"

"Nothin' to think. They got back what they been dishin' and they deserve that and more. But I won't be happy until I see them either in jail or dead," replied a very determined and revengeful Tabby. She had been dealt a bad hand with the bunch, not once, but twice, and she wanted no more of that. As she struck back against the one called Milo, she wanted the others to feel the same retaliation.

Cord dropped his eyes, trying his best to understand what she felt. It was one thing for him to want vengeance after what they did to his family, but another to want to retaliate in a personal way. She had been taken and manhandled, her pride stripped, her ability to defend herself taken from her, but she had struck out. Yet that was not enough for her, and Cord did his best to understand.

"It's gonna take a few days before I can do any riding, and we don't know for sure where those men have gone, or even if they left. So we must still be on our guard and take nothing for granted. After what you told me about the big one, Newt Morrison, it sounds like he wants you for himself, and a man like that does not give up easily."

"But the way Cadan described those that hit his claim and those that were wounded, it sounded to me like he was the first one that took a bullet."

"Could be, but we don't know for sure, nor do we know how bad he was hit. He could be lying dead somewhere in the trees, or...he could be planning his next claim jumping for him and his men."

"So, what do we do?"

"Well, you moved us from the other camp, and that's good, but Cadan found us easily and if they want to, they could also find us, so..." he shrugged.

"You think we should move our camp again?"

"The problem is, I won't be much help. But if we could move down that way," nodding to the draw to the north and at the bottom of the hill, "we'd be closer to the water and you wouldn't hafta lead the animals to water. I haven't seen it, but does it look like a good campsite?"

"It does," she glanced around where they were, "better'n this. And it is close to water. The only reason we didn't move further before was cuz you was too big to move!" she declared, grinning at Cord.

"Well, if I take it easy, I should be able to make it, maybe even lead my horse. If we can pack the stuff on 'em, it might be easier."

30

NURTURE

THE NEW CAMP WAS SITUATED PERFECTLY FOR PROTECTION
from the elements and from sight. With a thicket of
aspen on the back side, that was so dense it was
impossible for a horse to get through, and a steep
bluff that had been dug out by some long-ago
prospector on the far side, and open grasses that led
to the bottom of the draw below them and a spring-
fed feeder creek that provided ample fresh water, it
was a perfect place for Cord's recovery. They were
settling into their new camp, had just finished their
supper and doing the cleanup, when Blue came to
his feet, staring up the long draw and letting a low
growl come from his chest. Cord came to his knees,
lifted the binoculars and looked to see three moose
strolling into the valley bottom where several small
ponds and the bigger stream cut its way through.
Deep grasses were tall enough to tickle the bellies of
the big beasts and Cord saw it was a bull, a cow, and

a young cow, probably last year's calf. He chuckled as he handed the binoculars to Tabby, "Take a look. You've probably never seen them before."

Tabby frowned, lifted the binoculars, and a slow grin split her face, "Moose?"

"Ummhmm."

"Are they good eating?"

"Ummhmm."

"Should we try to get one?"

"Too big. It'd take you and me at least a couple months to eat that much meat, and I ain't in no condition to haul 'em down here to dress 'em out, and you're too little!" he chuckled.

"I ain't neither," grumbled Tabby, still watching the big dark moose as they waded into the water. "But they *are* big!"

"We'll wait, get us a deer or antelope or bighorn. That'll be a better size for just the two of us. There will probably be deer in that same draw either this evenin' or early mornin'. That'd be the time to get one."

"Even a deer is too big for the two of us," suggested Tabby, lowering the binoculars.

"Nah, we can keep the back strap, tenderloins, roasts, and smoke the rest."

"Smoke? You know how to do that?"

"Sure," he replied. "Done it before, not hard."

"Then maybe in the mornin' I'll get us a deer!" declared a determined Tabby, smiling.

———

She was out of her bedroll at the first hint of light in the eastern sky, the crest of the butte behind them rising high with its black timbered crown to make long shadows across the small draw that came from the east side of Bald Mountain. The early rays of sunlight danced across the ripples of the little pond below them and the long valley where they spotted the moose stretched westward as if fleeing from the rising sun.

But Tabby was already moving that direction, staying near the tree line of the aspen that skirted the pines on the flanks of the big Bald Mountain. When she saw movement, she dropped to one knee, lifted the binoculars for a look-see and spotted several mule deer tiptoeing to the little spring-fed creek. She waited, watching, guessing them to be a good hundred yards away, and when they were facing the creek, she slowly moved a little closer. When she was within about fifty yards, a big buck suddenly lifted his antlered head, big ears wide, and looked her direction, but she knew she was in tall grass and could not be easily distinguished, yet she did not move so much as an eyelash. Finally the buck relaxed, lowered his head, and stuck his nose in the water.

Tabby had her eyes on a young buck that showed only spikes for antlers, and he was behind the bigger buck, tiptoeing closer. Tabby slowly lifted her Winchester and took careful aim, the front ramp sight splitting the buckhorn sights at the rear. She took a deep breath, let some out, and slowly squeezed the trigger. The rifle bucked, blasted, and sent a lance of flame and smoke that chased the slug that flew true and buried itself in the low chest of the young buck. The deer sprang forward in shock, but crumpled in the grass, one last kick from his hind legs and he lay still. The others bounced away, their legs working like springs and within seconds, they melted into the trees without a sound.

Tabby lowered her rifle, smiling at her success, and slowly stood to crane and see the downed buck. She glanced back toward their camp but could see nothing, and she walked to her kill. There was always a little sadness in the first look at the dead animal, knowing she killed it, but there was also pride and satisfaction at the successful hunt. She looked around, ensuring there was no one near and dropped to one knee beside the carcass and began field dressing the animal. She split it from tail to chin, shook her head at the rising steam from the guts, took a deep breath, and reached in to pull out the entrails and more. She separated the liver and heart, pushed the gut pile aside, and went to the water to wash her hands and arms.

She looked up to see Cord coming atop a bareback Kwitcher and leading the mule. He was smiling and nodding as he neared, "I heard the shot, started to take a look but somebody stole my binoculars. But I guessed that this was what you were doin'," he chuckled.

Since he was not in shape to lift, and she was outweighed by the deer, Cord put a rope around the neck of the carcass, had Tabby hold the mule, and Cord, with Kwitcher's help, pulled the carcass onto the back of the mule where they tied it down and returned to camp to finish the butchering.

As they quartered the carcass, Cord suggested, "Alder is the best for smoking the meat. We'll build us a little fire there," nodding to the bigger trees, "under that spruce so it can filter out the smoke and we can use some of the branches to hold the strips of meat. We'll hang the rest up there," pointing to the biggest aspen, "out of reach of anything else."

"Well, we ain't hangin' ever'thing. I'm wantin' some venison roast with Indian potatoes and such," stated Tabby.

"Sounds almighty good to me!" replied a grinning Cord.

———

It was mid-morning when they finished quartering the deer, hung three-quarters high in an aspen, and cut a big roast from the rump of the fourth quarter. Tabby put the big roast in the Dutch oven that she would hang over the coals and use as a roasting pot, but Cord suggested, "Don't we need some carrots, potatoes, and onions for that roast?"

Tabby frowned, looking at him, "You expect me to go to town and get those just for your supper?"

"No, come with me and we'll go wilderness shopping!" he chuckled, stepping on a stump to get aboard Kwitcher. He gave Tabby a hand up and with Blue in the lead, the two rode from camp to the bottom of the draw where Cord started looking for the white blossoms of yampa and the tall stems of onion. When they neared the edge of some grasses near the creek, he spotted the blossoms, pointed them out, "Get a stick and dig around those roots. Those are what the Indians call Yampa or wild carrots." He had grabbed up a pouch and handed it to Tabby when she slid to the ground and grabbed up a stick and went to her knees to begin grubbing for roots. When she had a good bunch, she started to put them in the pouch, but Cord said, "Better wash 'em first, and over there's some onions!" he pointed to the heavy-hanging red-tipped bulbs on the tall skinny stems, "but when you dig 'em, be sure to smell 'em. If they don't smell like onions, throw 'em away. They look a lot like what they call *Death Camas*. And that's plum poisonous!"

She dug several onions, smelled them all and nodded as she stacked them nearby. She washed all the gatherings and looked up at Cord with a questioning expression. He answered with, "C'mon, we'll go on the hill yonder. It's sunny, dry, and rocky. Good place to find potatoes." She shook her head, accepting his hand up, and swung up behind him, holding tight to the pouch of vegetables.

Cord spotted a scattering of white blossoms and he pointed them out, "See those white blossoms, how they're shaped kinda like a potato and not flat like the Yampa or Camas. Dig around the roots of that, it's what the natives call Indian Potato."

She slid to the ground, dug several roots, put them in the pouch and stood on a big rock to swing aboard Kwitcher and the two rode back to camp. When she slid to the ground, she said, "What? There's no wild salt and pepper?"

"Prob'ly, I know there are some salt flats in places, but not around here. Pepper plants? Nah, don't know 'bout them."

Tabby shook her head, chuckling, as she finished preparing the roast with the new additions and soon had the covered pot hanging over the low burning fire which would soon be hot coals and they would lower the pot to simmer until ready. She looked at Cord, "Say, we didn't change your bandages this morning, guess we got too busy with the deer and such." She motioned to the blankets, "You stretch out there, I'll get the makins' and we'll get it done!"

Cord grinned, shook his head, "You sure are gettin' bossy!"

"You've been bossin' me around all mornin'! Now it's my turn!" she retorted, pointing to the blankets and scowling for him to stretch out and prepare to have his bandages changed. When she had stripped the bandages from his lower side and back, she was pleased with the progress, "That salve stuff is doin' a good job! You're healin' up purty good!"

"Why are you so surprised?" asked Cord. "It's common for the high mountain air to help when it comes to healing and the natives have been usin' that *stuff* as you call it, for a long time."

Tabby chuckled, "Well, yeah. I'm just glad it's doin' good." She looked at the bandage on the side of his head and began stripping it off. She looked closely at the deep gouge of the bullet's path, saw the scab, and was pleased with the healing, "I think we can leave that bandage off. Let the air get to it and I think it'll go well." She looked back at the other wounds, "But these," as she reached for the tin of salve, "need some more time and salve. Roll over on your side so I can tend to 'em."

She soon finished the bandaging, put the supplies away in the parfleche, and sat back. "Is it still pretty sore?"

"Yeah, but it's doin' better. Maybe another day or two and we can get outta here."

"And go where?"

"Well, I'd like to check out that cabin where they took you, just to be sure, and maybe we'll find something that'll tell us where they might be or where they went."

"For right now, how 'bout some rest till the roast is done and we can have supper?"

Cord grinned, chuckled as he stretched out, pulled his hat over his eyes, and folded his hands across his chest, and pretended to be asleep and snoring, but a grin was tugging at the corners of his mouth as he peeked from under the hat brim to see a grinning Tabby sitting back on her heels.

31

———

DIRECTION

Two days were spent de-boning the venison, smoking much of it into jerky, and giving the rest a good smoke to preserve it when they packed it into the panniers for traveling. There was nothing strenuous about the work, but it was necessary and the moving around helped strengthen the healing of Cord. As they sat about the simmering coals and watched the colors of the western sky while the sun was tucking itself away, Cord looked to Tabby. He thought she was a very pretty young woman, and she had grit and more of it than many men. She was definitely one to ride the river with, but he was hesitant to think of her in a romantic way, he had already become enamored with a woman, Yellow Singing Bird of the Capute Ute, and she had followed him, wanting to share his life, but they were attacked by the Jayhawkers and she was killed.

He shook his head at the memory, lifted his eyes

to Tabby, and did not want to have that happen to her, it just was not a safe place for any woman, not at his side. He had thought of her as a sister, a good friend, a companion, and did his best not to allow any thoughts of a commitment of any kind in the romantic way, but...he shrugged. Knowing that some things were not easily controlled and his mother had often told him, "Affairs of the heart are not easily understood, nor controlled. It's best to let the Lord give you guidance when it comes to that." But she never told him how to turn that control over to the Lord. He shook his head again, reached for the coffeepot, and looked her way.

She was grinning at him and asked, "What was going on in your mind that had you so frustrated? You were makin' faces, squirming, and such like you were having a nightmare, but you weren't asleep!"

"Oh, just thinkin'...I dunno." He lifted his cup to take a long drink, trying to think of something sensible to say, but words did not come. He sighed heavily, "I think we could leave in the mornin', if you want."

"And then what?"

"Well, I think we'll go to that cabin, look around for any sign. If we don't find any, maybe go down to the claim of Cadan, see him, see if he's heard anything. Then we'll decide...but I'm thinkin' we'll probably head toward Breckenridge. That is where you heard them say they might be goin', isn't it?"

Tabby nodded, sipping her own coffee. She

looked at Cord over the rim of the cup, lowered, it and asked, "I've noticed the way you've been looking at me, kinda funny like, I dunno. What's the matter, you havin' second thoughts about me comin' along?"

"Sorta. You remember I told you about Yellow Singing Bird, the Ute woman that was with me for a while, and that the Jayhawkers killed her."

"Yeah..."

"I don't want that happenin' to you."

"No, there's somethin' else. What'chu been thinkin' about me?"

Cord dropped his eyes, sat his coffee cup down and clasped his hands, his elbows on his knees as he leaned forward a little to look at her. "Well, I was thinkin' of you like a sister, like my sister, Marybel; you remind me of her a little. And I was thinkin' of you as a partner, you know, like a partner in a gold mine, or business, travelin' together and such. And I was thinkin' about you as a pretty woman that could be a heartbreaker," he chuckled, reaching to refill his coffee cup. "I'm not sure the two of us travelin' together is the right thing, you know, folks might talk and such. Maybe we need to be finding you a good home or..." he shrugged.

She dropped her eyes and her shoulders drooped. Cord shook his head as he looked at her. It looked like the air and life had just drained out of her, and he could tell she was hurt. She lifted her head, looked at him and all around the camp. She stood and walked around a little, then stopped before Cord and began, "Cord, you're all I've got. They killed my family, they killed my brothers, and then you came along, like a delivering angel or something." She stepped back a step, looked around and back to Cord, "I don't care if you think of me as your sister, your friend, your partner, or your lover. I don't care, but I've got to go with you. It's important to me to get those men—those men that killed my brothers and used me in the doin' of it! Those men that tried to take me the second time and were goin' to do...only the Lord knows what... and I can't sleep a wink, or anything else, until they are either locked up for life or dead in their graves. Maybe then I can think of something else and if you wanna get rid of me then, so be it. But please...not now."

Cord knew he had hurt her, just the mention of leaving her behind filled her with dread. He looked at her, into her eyes, and saw the fear, dread, and a hint of hopefulness. He stood, spread wide his arms and stepped close to her. She came into his arms and wrapped hers around his waist, he winced at the touch, and she pulled back, but he held her close and for the first time, this felt right.

They held each other for a moment, stepped apart and she wiped the tears from her eyes and Cord said, "We better turn in if we're leavin' in the mornin'."

She smiled, nodded, and turned toward her blankets.

—————

THEY WERE in the saddle before first light, taking the dim game trail through the trees that Tabby had followed from the captive cabin back to their camp. The trees were thick and the trail uncertain, but with Blue in the lead and followed closely by Kwitcher, they made progress through the trees and were soon at the tree line, looking across the clearing at the cabin. Behind the cabin was the caved in entrance to a mine shaft that had been worked some years past and now had as many weeds and wildflowers as rocks.

From where they sat, Tabby now beside Cord, he noticed what appeared to be two graves set back from the cabin. He frowned, looked at Tabby, "I thought Cadan said there was only one dead man, but that looks like two graves."

Tabby shrugged and glanced to Cord as he nudged Kwitcher forward. There was no sign of horses or any other life, but they moved cautiously, rifles in hand and lying across the pommels of their saddles. As they neared the cabin, Cord called out, "Hello the cabin! Come out with your hands high!" Nothing moved. Blue took a tentative step forward, looked back at Cord and at his wave, and the dog moved forward, his head down in an attack stance as he tiptoed toward the door. Cord called out again, "Hello the cabin! Come out with your hands high!" Again, nothing moved, no sound came. Cord glanced to Tabby and back to the door. He looked back at Tabby, "Keep your rifle ready, cover me if need be."

She nodded and lifted her rifle as Cord slipped to the ground. He stepped to the door, used the butt of his rifle and banged on the door, and yelled, "Open up!" Again, nothing moved. He glanced back to Tabby, then pulled the latch string, and pushed the door open. A rectangle of light sifted through the window, dust mites dancing, as Cord stepped inside. He looked around the one room cabin, saw a broken chair, two bunks that were a wreck, scattered debris including bloody bandages on the floor, and little else. He stepped outside, rifle hanging at his side. He looked to Tabby and shrugged, "Nothin'."

Cord walked around the side of the cabin and looked at the two graves, but there were no markers. He glanced to Tabby, "Don't stand to reason, two graves. Cadan said the outlaws left the dead man lay, but now two graves?"

Tabby shrugged and shook her head, "Maybe we can go down to Cadan's claim, talk to him."

"Yeah, but first I want to make a walk around, see if they left through the trees or somethin'." He kept his Winchester in hand and headed to the tree line by the trail where they came up, then started a slow walk within the tree line, looking for sign of the group leaving. The cabin faced to the east and Cord and Tabby had come from a trail on the north side. Now as he walked, he searched for any game trail that showed signs of horses or just fresh tracks of horses making their own trail. When he passed over the entry to the mine and moved further south, he could see the wagon road that came from Nevada City, although it had little use in the past few years, and it was on that road that the vigilantes came to the cabin. But the wagon road came from the east and made a sharp bend to the north to go to the cabin; that bend held thick trees on both sides, but as Cord neared, he saw a trail that came from the bend and into the trees.

He grinned, seeing the fresh sign of several horses taking the trail, probably yesterday sometime, but there were several. He frowned, went to one knee to look closer, and as near as he could tell there were five or six horses, maybe seven. But there were only three of the Jayhawkers left, at least of the bunch that had been raiding in this area. He stood, looking at the tracks and thinking, remembering others that were with them in Georgetown, the Yaqui and the one called Chapo, and there was another one, "*I think they called him Gooseneck,*" he mumbled. Then he turned back to the cabin. When he came near, he looked at Tabby, "Looks like they went through the trees yonder, I think that'll take 'em down to Idaho Springs or Clear Creek Canyon. But let's go down, talk to Cadan, 'fore we leave."

She handed Cord the reins from Kwitcher, slipped her rifle back in the scabbard, looked at Cord, nodded, "Then lead off, I'll follow." She smiled, watched him mount up, and they left the cabin behind and Tabby was remembering the first man she killed, right there. She nodded toward the grave, remembering the experience and not necessarily liking the thought. But she put it behind her, and moved beside Cord, smiled, and looked down the road, seeing it straighten out to the east with claims littering the hillsides.

32

TRAIL DUST

CADAN WAS BUSY AT HIS SLUICE WHEN CORD AND TABBY crossed the little creek. He stopped shoveling, came near, and yelled, "Mornin'! You're lookin' good, at least better than the last time I saw you."

Cord chuckled, "And top of the mornin' to you!" He leaned forward on his pommel and asked, "Say, did you or any of your men go up to that cabin up around the bend where those Jayhawkers were holed up?"

"Well, we went up there that time I told you about, but..." he paused, "Get down and come inside. I'm needin' some coffee. How 'bout you?"

"Sure," answered Cord, glancing to Tabby. They both stepped down, tied their mounts and the mule to the bit of a hitchrail that stood before Cadan's cabin, and they followed him inside. He motioned to the table and brought cups and the pot, poured the cups full, sat the pot down and seated himself.

"So, yesterday we saw three riders, not miners, two Mexican looking types, you know, dark complected and wearing those short jackets and big hats, and another one that looked almost like a stick man, he was so long and skinny. They didn't even look our way, rode right on by, and never saw 'em come back. They either stayed at the cabin with the others, or..." and shrugged as he lifted his coffee.

Cord frowned, thinking and remembering. The description of the riders made him think of three men that had ridden with the Jayhawkers back in Georgetown, but he thought they had chosen to go their own way. He remembered their names, one was called Yaqui, he had brought Malcolm's horse to him, and his partner was Chapo. The skinny one might be the one they called Gooseneck. He looked at Cadan, "We also saw two graves beside the cabin, we know of the one, but the other?"

"Probably one of the two we wounded when they attacked my claim. One of those was the one I thought was the leader, a big man, built like a barrel and broad shouldered, big head, just a big man. The other'n, well, he made me think of a mouse. But he was grinnin' and had a mouthful of rotten teeth! Other'n that, can't tell you much."

Cord nodded, sipped his coffee and glanced to Tabby, then back to Cadan. Cadan asked, "You goin' after 'em?"

Cord nodded, "Ummhmm. Looks like they took a trail through the trees, the trail takes off from the road at the sharp bend right 'fore it gets to the cabin."

Cadan nodded, "Ummhmm, that'll take 'em down to York Gulch, on to Fall River and down to the stage road that goes through Clear Creek Canyon. They could go to Idaho Springs or..." he shrugged, taking another drink of his coffee.

Cord nodded toward Tabby, "She heard 'em say somethin' about goin' to Breckenridge, so we might just head thataway."

"Uh, you might want to re-think that. If they're goin' where the mines or claims are, they will probably head up Sanderson Pass or some call it Snake River pass. It leads to Montezuma and there's been silver strikes all up and down that mountain and more. There's more activity there than Breckenridge."

"It that closer?"

"Ummhumm, you go through Georgetown, keep goin' through Silver Plume, and you'll see a road, prob'ly some signs that take you up Sanderson Pass and o'er to Montezuma. Course if you get there and nothin's happenin', you can still go on to Breckenridge."

———

ALTHOUGH IT WAS CALLED Bald Mountain, it was neither bald nor much of a mountain. Sitting in the shadows of the real granite tipped peaks of the Front

Range, Bald Mountain was just a big hill but it served
as a landmark for the many prospectors in the area.
The trail of the men Cord called Jayhawkers, flanked
the south skirts of the big hill and meandered
through the black timber. Cord had Blue take the
trail and Cord and Tabby rode one after the other on
the narrow trail. They had gone less than a half mile
when the trees thinned and they crested a slight rise
that afforded a good look at the hills and valleys
beyond. Cord reined up, waited as Tabby pulled
alongside and he nodded to the trail that rode the
ridge but turned to the south. "That'll take us to
Idaho Springs; that lays in the bottom of that long
valley. You can see the wagon road coming up this
gulch and all the prospect holes that scar the
hillsides."

He leaned forward and pointed to the ground,
"You can see their tracks, looks to be five or six, and
they're headed down thataway, prob'ly goin' to
town, get supplies or..." he shrugged. "But if they're
goin' to Breckenridge like you heard, or Montezuma
like Cadan thinks, they'll come back up," he stood in
his stirrups and pointed to the long break in the
timbered mountains and ridges, "They'll go through
the Clear Creek Canyon. That'll take 'em to Georgetown, and on to the other places. We can either
follow 'em to Idaho Springs, but any confrontation
there could get a little crowded, or," he leaned
forward again, "we can cut through the trees and
drop into that gulch, I think that's York Gulch that

Cadan mentioned, and take it and the other'n down to Clear Creek and get ahead of 'em. Then we could either wait for 'em along the way, or go on to Georgetown and Montezuma and be ready and waitin' for 'em."

Tabby listened and watched, stood in her stirrups to see a little better, dropped into her saddle and leaned on the pommel, "So, if we follow them, and they know we're followin', they could pick the time and place for the battle. But..." she paused, looked around at the trail, the gulch below, and the canyon beyond, "if we get ahead of 'em, then we can pick the time and place, right?"

Cord grinned, nodded, "Ummhmm. You're right."

She smiled, "Does that help you decide?"

Cord chuckled, and nudged Kwitcher to the dim game trail that took them away from following the others and pointed them to a slight swale and a gulch beyond that appeared to lead to the bigger valley below. Cord waved Blue to the trail and he trotted off, tail wagging, tongue lolling, and trotting at his chosen pace.

———

"WE'RE GOIN' to Idaho Springs - I gotta find me a doctor. This bullet hole's gettin' infected," growled Newt Morrison as he swung aboard his big bay gelding.

The others were mounting up and Buck Smithers asked, "How can ya tell it's gettin' infected?" He settled in his saddle, nudging his paint gelding alongside the big man.

"Cuz it stinks!" growled Newt, lifting the bandage to look. The bullet had torn through his shoulder muscle, just above the collarbone and tore a big chunk of muscle with it. He looked at the wound, winced, and made a face.

Coogan moved beside Newt, opposite Smithers, and said, "How can you tell? You ain't took a bath in months and you're purty ripe your own self!"

Newt swung his arm to backhand Coogan, but the mouthy man was on his bad side and Newt hurt himself as he tried to strike Coogan. He growled, "Keep it up and you'll be wantin' a doctor yourself, or maybe an undertaker!" Newt nudged his mount away from the cabin. It was because of the smell that Newt had insisted the other two men dig graves for Milo Slater and James Flood, who had died from his wounds suffered when they attacked the claims and were hit by the vigilantes. There were no markers at the graves, Morrison had only been concerned about the smell and neither conscience nor commitment had caused the men to go to the trouble of digging the graves.

As they rode from the cabin, they heard horses coming and they left the road on the uphill side, taking cover in the trees. With rifles at the ready, expecting vigilantes, the three were ready to open fire when Newt said, "Hold your fire!" and hollered at the riders, "Hey! Yaqui! Chapo! Gooseneck! You lookin' for us?" Newt motioned to Coogan and Smithers as he nudged his mount from the trees. He was laughing, "I never thought we'd be seein' you three again!"

"Ah, chihuahua! We heard about some Jayhawkers that were raidin' claims and thought you might need a hand!" answered Yaqui, pushing his sombrero to the back of his head.

"You came at the right time! We were just leavin'. Goin' to find me a doctor, then we're headin' to some prime country. Lotsa claims, good gold, no law!"

"Sounds good, but why you leavin' here?"

"Vigilantes! They shot us up, killed four men, wounded me, and they outnumber us ten to one, so..." he shrugged, "Come on, ride along, an' we'll talk!" declared Newt, glad to see the numbers on his side. He was already thinking about what they would do at Georgetown and places west. He could smell the gold already. He chuckled to himself, winced at the pain in his shoulder, but took to the trail.

33

DESTINY

"Do you know who those men are that joined the others?" asked Tabby, the trail that dropped into the gulch was wide enough for them to ride side by side, and she looked at Cord as she had been thinking and wondering about their journey.

"Not sure, I think they might be some that were with them before they hit Black Hawk and Nevada City. There were several more when they were around Georgetown, but they split up and hightailed it when they ran into a little trouble."

"What kinda trouble?"

"Oh, they decided to get a new sheriff, one that would do a better job."

Tabby frowned, thinking about people, looked at Cord and asked, "Why is it that evil people always find others of their kind. It seems that no matter where we've been, there were always those that tried to push others around, take whatever they wanted, do whatever they wanted, just evil!" she fumed, frustration showing with her every expression and move. As her horse picked his way down the twisting trail, Tabby rocked back and forth on her saddle, her hips moving in cadence with the steps of the big sorrel, Cassi. She looked to Cord, waiting an answer.

Cord chuckled and answered, "That's a question that has hung over mankind ever since the Garden of Eden. It seems there will always be evil, it's kinda like, well, cold and heat, light and darkness, good and evil. It's not so much the presence of one, but the absence of the other. When men don't have God in their lives, evil fills the vacuum. When families shun the things of God and try to go through life without the Creator of life, they find life to be more difficult than God planned, because evil raises its ugly head and whispers about how things could be if you didn't have to have laws, if you could just do whatever you want, take whatever you want, run right over everybody else, how much easier it would be, but that's a lie of the devil himself, and if you notice, the word devil is D, with evil attached!"

Tabby frowned, "Hmmm, but—"

"Let me continue," interrupted Cord. "See, it's like cold, is it the cold or the absence of heat? And darkness, is it dark or the absence of light? Whenever you light a fire, cold retreats. And darkness, whenever you bring light, darkness recedes. The same is true with evil, when good men stand for what is right, like the vigilantes did back at Nevada Gulch, evil ran away. But for evil to stay away, good men must continue to do what is right, even when it is inconvenient or uncomfortable or difficult. And that's where many fail, they're willing to stand up as a group in one instance, but to continue to do so, requires a greater commitment than many are willing to make."

"Sounds tiring," replied Tabby.

"Anything worth doing is worth doing right. Life has ways of reminding us of that, you know, like taking a bath, then we get dirty again, take a bath again, and so on and so on."

"But you said evil was the absence of good. Why doesn't God just come down and wipe out evil once and for all, and let the good prevail?"

"He did that once, when He sent His son Jesus to die on the cross for our sins. But God's way is to use people. People like you and me, to tell others, show others what belief is and show them what His love is, and that good that takes over the lives of people will dispel the evil that is all about us. That's why we must stand against evil every time and every place we confront it. The only thing it takes for evil to run rampant, is for good people to do nothing."

The trail they followed was in the bottom of York Gulch and it opened to the Fall River draw. Cord reined up, leaned on the pommel and looked up and down the gulch. Tall ponderosa stretched their hoary heads above the spruce and fir, the aspen fluttered their leaves as if greeting the travelers and the rough barked cottonwoods stood sentinel over the creek banks. The chuckling of the creek as the water cascaded over the rocks told of a pure water that probably hid some speckled brook trout and maybe some rainbow trout. Cord grinned, "We haven't come too far, but that's more'n I've ridden in a good while. Maybe we oughta make camp, do a little fishing, have some fresh trout for supper, what say?"

Tabby giggled, "I've never caught trout before. The only fish that had enough patience to wait for me was catfish!"

"Then we'll have some fun catching these tasty trout. I've got some gear that'll do the job, but first, let's set us up a camp, over there on the other side where there's more trees for cover." He nodded to a small clearing on the far side, nudged Kwitcher into the water and Blue jumped in to swim against the current and make his way across the creek. With the water no more than a couple feet deep except in deeper pools that cut into the bank, the cold water splashed and laughed as the little group crossed over. When the horses climbed the far bank, they stopped, shook and almost unseated Tabby, who grabbed the saddle horn with a squeal and a giggle.

They slipped to the ground, stripped the gear from the horses and let them have a good roll in the grass, then picketed the horses and mule within reach of the backwater at the bend and ample grass for graze. Cord stacked the panniers, parfleches, and more at the base of a big ponderosa, rolled out their bedrolls nearby and began gathering firewood and rocks for a fire circle. They soon had the coffee pot dancing and Cord sat nearby fidgeting with the gear to be used for trout fishing. He grinned up at Tabby, held out a willow with a long string attached and a wiggling worm on a hook. "Here ya go! Now, see where the creek makes that bend and the water has cut away under the bank on the curve? Drop your hook in the water just upstream of the curve, let it bounce along the bottom to that undercut and wait for a bite."

"And then what?"

"Well, pull it in! Can't eat 'em if we don't catch 'em!" he declared, laughing and finishing his own line and hook.

Tabby caught a nice silvery looking trout on the first cast, pulled him in and dropped him on the grass as she stumbled backward and fell flat. She was squealing and laughing as Cord came running and unhooked the fish, tossing it further from the stream in the grass. He chuckled, "Good job, reckon we *will* have somethin' for supper after all!"

"I've got mine, you go catch yours!" declared a laughing Tabby, her arms stretched behind her, propping her up as she laughed with Cord.

They continued their fishing for another hour or more, finally after catching six nice pan-sized trout, Cord came to Tabby, held up his two to her four and said, "Time to clean 'em and get ready for supper!"

Tabby grinned, looked at her four lying side by

side in the grass, compared them to his two and made a face, laughed, and said, "Not bad for a beginner!"

"Oh, I had plenty of others, but I let 'em go, din't wanna show you up. That's not gentlemanly," he chuckled. They walked back to their camp and stopped as they entered the clearing. Sitting on the log beside the fire, holding a cup of steaming coffee, was an Indian. His stoic expression unchanging when they came near. He nodded as they dropped the fish nearby, looked at their catch, and said, "Good. We eat."

"Uh, who are you and what are you doing here?"

"I am Long Walker, I am Weenuchiu Ute. This is my land," he waved both arms around to indicate all the land where they camped. "But you are good people, you may stay in my land. We will eat together."

The old man was dressed in buckskins, fringed leggings with intricate beadwork going the length of the leggings next to the fringe. A buckskin vest, also adorned with fringe and extensive beadwork. A bone horn pipe breastplate hung over his chest, and a three-tiered bone hair-pipe choker covered his neck. His long braids showed strips of grey, and his weathered face was covered with wrinkles. But on his head was a weather-beaten high crowned felt hat that looked a bit out of place, but the wide brim shaded his eyes and he nodded as he spoke.

Cord sat down opposite the man and said, "I

knew some of the Capute Ute, down in the San Luis Valley. I was friends with the daughter of the chief, Kaniache."

"Was she your woman?"

"Yes, until she was killed."

"It is hard to lose a good woman. My woman was with me a long time. We had many little ones..." his eyes appeared to glaze over as he remembered his family. He shook his head, looked back at Cord, "But she is gone now. The people said I was old, and I should leave. It was time for me to walk with my ancestors." He paused again, looked down at the glowing coals in the fire pit, lifted his eyes to Cord and let a slow grin split his face before he said, "But they were not ready for me, so I left."

Cord chuckled "Your ancestors were not ready for you?"

"No, they told me to go away and come back another time. Maybe then they would be ready. They were old women, too many old women. None were my old woman." He grunted, shook his head, and drank the last of his coffee. He stood up, standing quite tall and straight, looked around and glanced to Cord, "I go get my horse now. I will be back to eat." He walked into the trees.

Cord chuckled, "Didn't know we was havin' comp'ny. Did'chu?"

"Well, I'm glad *I* caught enough fish for all of us. If I left it up to you, you would have to do without!" she giggled, working with the fish and the frying pan. She had cleaned the fish, cut off the heads, and rolled them in cornmeal. She had the frying pan at the edge of the fire and as the bacon grease melted, she lay a couple fish in the pan and began frying their supper. She had stuffed several of the Indian potatoes in the hot coals and had made some pan bread that she would cook as soon as she was done with the fish. Cord looked at Tabby, smiled, and nodded, "You're gettin' to be pretty handy to have around!"

She grabbed a pine cone and threw it at him, laughing as he ducked and fell off the log.

Long Walker shared their supper, talked with them about the area and his people and told of some "...bad white men that smell. Camped near the river beyond the stage stop, I think they will rob the stage or..." He spent the night with them, but was gone before first light, leaving behind nothing but the memory.

Tabby looked at Cord, "I liked him. It would have been good to have him with us. We could learn a lot from him."

"Ummhmm, but I think he's gone looking for his ancestors. Maybe now they'll let him stay."

34

WEST

THE WERE SITTING BY THE FIRE, THE SUN WAS JUST beginning to show itself as it stretched shadows down the long Clear Creek Canyon. Their camp was just upstream on the Fall River and the grey light of early morning was making silhouettes of the long timber-covered ridge that stood tall on the eastern edge of the valley. Cord had spent his time on the rocky outcropping on the hill behind their camp, looking across the valley and talking with his Lord. He had been struggling with many things, becoming more contemplative since he had been joined in his quest by Tabitha. It was one thing for him to be driven by his quest for vengeance and to pursue those called Jayhawks, Red Legs, and Bush-whackers, that had left a trail of blood from Missouri across the young land of America and into the Rocky Mountains. But it was quite another for him to allow this young woman, alone in the world, to have her life shaped and marred by what had become an almost endless chase of outlaws and their evil ways.

He had also made a promise to Marshal Shaffen-burg and Marshal Cook when he was appointed as a federal marshal. That promise was to keep in touch, keep them apprised of his progress, and his plans. And he had yet to report anything to them. He had considered sending a letter, or even a telegram, and had also considered going back to Denver to report in to them. But, he did not want to lose the rest of the Jayhawker gang and if he left now, they could end up anywhere and do any number of things, none of which would be beneficial to anyone but themselves.

"What's troubling you? You look, well, upset," asked Tabby, pouring him some fresh coffee.

He looked up at her, sat with his elbows on his knees, cradling the hot cup of coffee in his hands, and looked down at the coffee. He was quiet for a moment, then looked up at her again and began to explain his consternation. "It was because of Cracker and Densmore back in Oro City that I got the appointment as marshal, and they were thinking I'd stay around and enforce the law there, Oro City and such, but when the outlaws left, I just had to follow. And I had also promised to keep in touch with Marshal Shaffenburg and Marshal Cook, you know, give a report on my work and chase after the outlaws, but I haven't sent so much as a letter. And now..." he shrugged, sipped some coffee, looked back at her and continued, "I haven't been too good at keeping my word to those men, none of 'em."

"Maybe you need to go into Idaho Springs, send a telegram. Or...you could wait until we get to Georgetown, there's a telegram there, isn't there?"

"Yeah, I think so." He stretched out his cup for a refill and Tabby accommodated him, smiling and waiting for him to continue. "And since there's only one of the original gang left, do I really want to continue this chase? And is it right for me to take you with me?"

"Not that again! I thought we settled that!" she declared. She sat down the coffee pot, stood, hands on hips and kicked at the dust. She looked down at the seated Cord, "Look, if my staying with you is going to keep on bothering you, maybe I'll just push on by myself. I've already shot one of 'em, maybe I can get some more. I can shoot as good as you, I can ride as good as you, I can *fish* better'n you! What do I need you for!" she glowered at him, kicked a couple rocks and a stick, mumbling to herself.

Cord looked at her, chuckled to himself and shook his head. "You're right. I'll send a telegram in Georgetown, wait to see what they say, then we'll decide. He might have something entirely different he wants me to be doin' instead of chasin' these no-goods!"

"And if he wants you to go after somebody else, what about me?"

"Hah! You ain't gettin' rid o' me that easy! What would I do when I get hungry for trout?"

She picked up a stick and threw it at him, both of them laughing as they cavorted. Cord motioned to the horses and they went to the animals to saddle up and get started on this next leg of their journey. When they entered the canyon of Clear Creek, the sun was warm on their backs and Clear Creek was crashing and cascading, white water splashing and the muted roar echoed off the canyon walls, magnifying the sound. But it was a pleasant sound, the natural sound of the land. They found a stretch of easy water, pushed their mounts into the stream and with the current pushing against them and the water just over knee high in these shallows, they made an easy crossing.

Once on the stage road, the horses shook but kept moving, and Cord laughed as Blue rolled in the grass at the edge of the road, trying to dry off. He quickly reclaimed his place in the lead of the group and bounded away, happy to be back on the trail. Cord pointed across the canyon at some high rock cliff faces. A small herd of big horn sheep were cavorting about, young ones bounding from rock to rock, showing their unbelievable footing as they seemingly bounced from one shear face to another, never missing a step and proud mothers watching on with an occasional glance to the big rams with massive full curl horns that stood stoic on the rock high above, surveying their domain and their family.

Tabby said, "Those are Big Horns, aren't they?"

Cord nodded and Tabby added, "Those are the first I've seen. They're magnificent!"

Cord grinned, nudged Kwitcher to move, and they continued on the trail. It was about ten miles to Georgetown and they should easily make it by mid-afternoon, but he was in no hurry. His idle thoughts reminding him of his struggle between vengeance and justice. But if he reported in to the marshal, maybe the scales would shift to justice, maybe...

"Didn't Long Walker say he saw some men that he said were bad men?"

"Ummhumm."

"Did he say where they were?"

"Ummhmm, somewhere along this road. He said he thought they were going to try to rob the stage."

"Shouldn't you, as a federal marshal, do something about that?"

"Maybe," he responded, shaking his head, trying to remember everything Long Walker had told them. Then he remembered, "He said they were camped by the river, past the stage stop."

"Where's the stage stop?"

"The Mill City House at Mill City."

"How far's that?"

"Oh, we might stop there for lunch!" Cord chuckled, twisting in his saddle to look back at Tabby.

The Mill City House set just off the stage road, with a barn out back and a big corral, the hotel/tavern/stage stop was a rarity in the area. With half the log building being two stories and held the hotel rooms and the kitchen and dining room on the ground floor, the other half stretched out to the side and was just a little more than one story and housed the tavern, and some loft rooms for overflow sleeping. When Cord and Tabby rode up to the place, a matronly woman was standing in the front door, an apron covering her front and she was wiping her hands on the apron skirt. She waved at the couple as they rode up, "Mornin' an' welcome! Hitch your horses there at the rail on the side and come on in, got coffee on and lunch'll be ready in a jiffy! The stage should be pullin' in shortly! C'mon in!" She turned and went back inside.

Cord grinned at Tabby, "You hungry?"

"Oh, maybe a little. Only cuz I don't hafta eat my own cooking," she said as she slid to the ground. They slapped reins around the hitchrail and tied the pack mule, and walked around to the front to enter the big log building. As they stepped inside, they had to stop and let their eyes get used to the dim light.

The woman motioned them to a table and said, "I'm Mabel Wilson, this is my place," she smiled, waving her free hand around to take in the entire building. "And dependin' on how many's on the stage, they usually take up all the rest o' them tables. But you'll get yours first an' they can do with what's left." She laughed and poured cups of coffee from a big coffee pot that took two hands to handle.

Mabel had just waddled away when the door

slapped open and three men pushed in, looking around and scowling at Cord and Tabby. "Where's the woman?" growled the man in front, his hand resting on the butt of his holstered pistol.

Cord nodded to the kitchen and lifted his coffee cup for a sip. He watched the men, used the cup to shield his lips and whispered to Tabby, "There's trouble—don't do anything unless I do. Keep your hands on the table and act like nothin's wrong."

Tabby turned slightly to look at Cord, glanced back to the men and reached for her coffee cup. As she lifted it, Mabel came from the kitchen, two plates of food before her and a broad smile for her guests. She nodded to the men, "Go 'head and take a table gents. Stage'll be along any minute now." She turned her attention back to Cord and set the plates down, glanced to the men and asked, "You fellas gonna be seated? Want sumpin' to eat?"

"No! We ain't gonna be seated an' we ain't eatin'. You sit down there," pointing to the table with Cord and Tabby, "wit' them others." The man had drawn his pistol and was waving it toward the table as he told the woman to be seated. "We're waitin' for the stage an' don' want none o' you interferin'! Unnerstan'?" he growled.

"Answer me! You unnderstan'?" he shouted at the three of them.

Cord lifted both hands shoulder-high, "We understand. Just be careful with that thing, I ain't anxious to get shot, nosiree!" He tried his best to look scared and nudged Tabby to do as he did and lift her hands. "Alright if'n we go 'head an' eat. Food gets cold in this high country!"

"Go 'head. Just don' get no idees!" growled the man. He lowered his voice and talked with the others. One man went outside, the other went to the window. The man at the window turned, "It's comin'!" he declared as he pulled his pistol and lifted his neckerchief to cover his face. The apparent boss of the group lifted his neckerchief as well, and with one last glare toward Cord and Tabby, he moved to the door to look out the window.

The rattle of trace chains and rumble of wheels blended with the thunder of a six-up team of horses as the stage arrived in a cloud of dust. The driver hollered, "Whoooaaa up there! Whoa now." As the stage pulled to a stop, he relaxed and leaned around to shout at the people inside. The driver was on the near side and the shotgunner was to his left. The driver said, "Everybody out! We're stoppin' for lunch! Outhouse aroun' back!"

As the commotion caught the attention of the two outlaws at the door and window, Cord nodded to Tabby, motioned to the man at the window, and he slowly rose, pulling his pistol as he did, and stepped behind the man at the door as Tabby did the same with the man at the window. She watched Cord, and as Cord lifted his pistol and brought it down on the back of the man's head, the man crumpled to the floor. Tabby did the same with the man at the window, even though she had to stand on tiptoes to reach high enough to strike the man's head.

Both outlaws were out cold on the floor. Cord looked at Mabel, "You got something you can tie these two up with?"

"Yes, yes, but what about the other'n?"

Cord grinned, looked to Tabby, and motioned to Mabel, "Give her a hand. I'm goin' after the other one." He had seen the man go around the side of the house where the horses were tethered and he asked, "There a back door?"

"Yes!" she replied and waved her hand, "Thru the kitchen!"

Cord quickly went through the kitchen and slowly worked his way around the corner of the building. The third outlaw was standing in the shadow between the hitchrail and the building and Cord casually walked to the horses and glanced to the man, "You waitin' for someone?" he asked as he fiddled with his gear on Kwitcher.

"How'd you get out here?" he asked, glancing from Cord to the stage. "Where's those two that was with me?"

"They're detained," said Cord as he lifted his pistol. The man turned back to look at Cord, his eyes flared and he spun on his heel, bringing the rifle to bear, but Cord's pistol roared and spat death, dropping the man in a clump at the end of the hitchrail. The blast made the horses jerk, but neither moved away, they were not afraid of the gunshot, having experienced it before from the hand of Cord. Blue came from under Kwitcher and leaned against Cord for some attention, just as the shotgunner came running around the corner, coach gun at the ready.

"What happened?" and looked down at the man. "You do this?"

"Ummhmm."

"Why?"

"He and his two partners inside were goin' to rob the stage."

"Oh, oh, well..." he stammered and turned to holler at the driver, "Hey Tubs! C'mere! These guys was gonna rob the stage an' this fella stopped 'em!"

————

CORD AND TABBY stood together watching the stage pull away. The two outlaws, tied and gagged, lay atop the stage and would be turned over to the sheriff in Georgetown. The driver had chuckled, "They just bilt 'em a new jail! They'll be tickled to put these two behind bars, but not as happy as I am they're goin'! Who should I say done it?"

"Oh, just a couple interested folks. Thanks for takin' 'em, Tubs!"

They waved as the driver turned back and nodded as he pulled out onto the road. The fresh team kicked up some dust as they turned onto the road and disappeared in the cloud of dust. Cord turned back to Tabby, "So, think that might be a hint as to what I'm s'posed to be doin', bein' a marshal or chasin' Jayhawkers?"

"I'm not sure which one is safer, but I kinda like you bein' a marshal," Tabby replied, smiling and drawing closer to him, slipping her hand through his arm.

Cord chuckled, shaking his head and grinning. *Maybe marshalin' would be more interestin'.*

A LOOK AT:
THE COVENANT

From the bestselling author of The Plainsman Western series comes a 2024 Independent Press Award Distinguished Favorite for Historical Fiction—an exciting and explosive new Western series.

It is a time of uncertainty in the infancy of a growing nation. The Wild West is open and beckoning to displaced men and families, many of whom choose to travel to the unsettled frontier, dreaming of new homes, land, and even riches. But few reckon on those who have lived in those lands for centuries—the native peoples. Blackfoot, Crow, Sioux, and more.

Elijah McCain, fresh from the Union army where he attained the rank of Lieutenant Colonel with the Mounted Rifles—a cavalry unit under General Sherman—has returned home to find his wife on her deathbed, pleading for her twin sons. She elicits a promise, a covenant, from her husband: "Find our boys, and bring them home."

So, Eli vows to do just that. Holding her hand as she slips from life, he promises to bring their sons home—no matter what. Even if it's the undoing of dreams, lives, and more.

AVAILABLE NOW

ABOUT THE AUTHOR

Born and raised in Colorado into a family of ranchers and cowboys, B.N. Rundell is the youngest of seven sons. Juggling bull riding, skiing, and high school, graduation was a launching pad for a hitch in the Army Paratroopers. After the army, he finished his college education in Springfield, MO, and together with his wife and growing family, entered the ministry as a Baptist preacher.

With many years as a successful pastor and educator, he retired from the ministry and followed in the footsteps of his entrepreneurial father and started a successful insurance agency, which is now in the hands of his trusted nephew. Having finally realized his life-long dream, B.N. has turned his efforts to writing a variety of books, from children's picture books and young adult adventure books, to the historical fiction and Western genres, which are his first loves.

Made in the USA
Coppell, TX
03 October 2024

38167334R00173